The Book of

T0246963

SMAN

K.E. Semmel

A Novel

sfwp.com

Library of Congress Cataloging-in-Publication Data
Names: Semmel, K. E., author.
Title: The book of Losman / K. E. Semmel.
Description: Santa Fe : Santa Fe Writers Project, 2024. | Summary: "Meet
    Daniel Losman-an American in Copenhagen, translating books and living
    a solitary existence. His longtime girlfriend has left him, and the only
    highlights in his life are encounters with an offbeat artist he thinks
    he's in love with and weekends with his three-year-old son, whom he
    worries has inherited his Tourette syndrome. When Losman learns of a
    new drug designed to locate the root of his Tourette through childhood
    memories, he's lured by promises of a cure and visits the mysterious lab
    that developed the drug. Initially, what he discovers buried deep within
    his brain rejuvenates him. But the more Losman takes the drug, the
    more he needs it. Losman steals some of the pills and locks himself away
    in his apartment, only to quickly find himself trapped inside his own
    mind. There's a way out of his head, but it will come at a price... With
    intelligence and humor reminiscent of Matt Haig's The Midnight Library,
    The Book of Losman explores the depths one man will go to piece himself
    together"—Provided by publisher.
Identifiers: LCCN 2023050377 (print) | LCCN 2023050378 (ebook) |
    ISBN 9781951631376 (trade paperback) | ISBN 9781951631383 (ebook)
Subjects: LCGFT: Novels.
Classification: LCC PS3619.E485 B66 2024 (print) | LCC PS3619.E485 (ebook) |
    DDC 813/.6—dc23/eng/20231218
LC record available at https://lccn.loc.gov/2023050377
LC ebook record available at https://lccn.loc.gov/2023050378

Published by SFWP
369 Montezuma Ave. #350
Santa Fe, NM 87501
www.sfwp.com

For Pia, who knows what went into this book,
and Esben, who will one day.

"For hende er ord ligesom snefnug, smukke og kolde,
de forsvinder hurtigere end man kan gribe dem. "

"Words are like snowflakes to her, beautiful and cold,
they vanish faster than you can catch them."

—Merete Pryds Helle, *Folkets skønhed*
(translated from Danish by Daniel P. Losman)

"Without the binding force of memory, experience
would be splintered into as many fragments as there
are moments in life. Without the mental time travel
provided by memory, we would have no awareness
of our personal history, no way of remembering the
joys that serve as the luminous milestones of our
life. We are who we are because of what we learn
and what we remember."

—Eric R. Kandel, *In Search of Memory*

Part I

Kramer is Dead

1

WHEN HE MOVED TO COPENHAGEN with his Danish girlfriend, Kat, fifteen years ago, Losman imagined his life like a Fodor's guidebook, rich with possibility and adventure. But it didn't turn out that way because no life ever did. And now that Kat had left him, he lived alone, except on the weekends his son, Aksel, visited. Losman was a literary translator. On an average day, he woke up, made coffee, and got to work filling Word documents with letters. Ten pages a day, that was his goal. On *this* particular day he would discover a dead man, punch a swan to save a little girl, and find an experimental memory study that would alter his life (and possibly his brain chemistry) forever. Not an average day at all. But at this moment, all that was in the near future. Now, in the present, he sat at his desk gaping at his fuzzy computer screen, having made it through six tedious pages of translation—when he was startled by a knock at his door.

It was a soft, hesitant rap, as if whoever was knocking was sorry to interrupt. Losman wasn't sure what he'd heard was real or imagined. But it left him momentarily breathless with anticipation. A visitor? Did he have a visitor? He cocked his ear to listen. And he heard it again, louder. Definitely a knock.

"*Et øjeblik!*" he said, standing abruptly. He rummaged the floor for his pants and slid them on as he stumbled across the room.

When he opened the door, he found his upstairs neighbor, Caroline Jensen, standing on the landing dressed in a green gabardine coat and a cloche hat. "Yes?" he said.

"Herre Kramer fell," she said, pointing a slender finger up the stairwell. Two flights above lived a crotchety old man named Kramer, an overweight, alcoholic, former postman Losman didn't care for. Losman stared at Caroline's jet-black fingernails. "How do you know he fell?"

"I heard a loud thud last night when I was making coffee."

"Last *night*?" Losman said.

"Can you help?"

He glanced at his laptop behind him. He still had four pages to translate, and he didn't like to step away from his day's work prematurely; the anxiety it caused him would swell like a tumor and increase his tics. But he knew that he couldn't say no, not to Caroline Jensen.

He followed her up the stairs like an obedient puppy. Nervous and anxious, his Tourette besting him like the lord and master it was, he squelched an urge to jerk his head and blow out a noisy puff of air. When they reached Kramer's door, she raised her hand and knocked. "Herre Kramer?" she said. "Herre Kramer? Won't you open up?"

There was no answer.

"I assume you don't have a key?" Losman said.

She shook her head.

"Maybe he's not home?"

"He's home." Caroline nodded at the long rectangular mail slot that was a staple in old apartment buildings like this. "See for yourself."

Losman squatted. He took a deep breath, pushed his index finger through the slot, and lifted the lid. A decadent odor pungent of cigarettes and feces stung his eyes and mouth. He flinched, pulling his hand away from the slot and gasping for air.

"Did you see him?"

"Not yet," he coughed. After covering his mouth and nose with his left bicep, he lifted the lid one more time. Holding his breath, he now saw a mountain of letters and magazines and newspapers piled on the floor. Losman scanned the room. What he was looking at was an apartment that was the perfect replica of his own, only in reverse. There was a recliner, a sofa, and a coffee table. At the far end, straight ahead, a wall yellowed by cigarette smoke divided the living room from the galley kitchen behind it. And there Losman saw a pair of unmoving legs sprawled out on the floor in the hallway, surrounded by broken glass; the other half of Kramer's body was lying on the kitchen linoleum, out of sight.

Losman got to his feet. "You better call somebody," he said to Caroline, wanting desperately to shake his head or clear his throat or blink or snort. "I think Kramer is dead."

AFTER SHE MADE THE CALL, they sat down on the stairwell to wait for the ambulance. Caroline was withdrawn, and Losman wondered what in the world had possessed her to wear a green gabardine coat and cloche hat. On her feet, he noted, she wore pink and white Nikes. No socks. Should he put his arm around her to comfort her? Probably not. He barely knew her. How then could he reassure Caroline without making her uncomfortable? Tell her it was all right? What he *wanted* to say was: If you heard Kramer fall last night, why did you wait until now to do anything? But that, he knew, was very much the wrong thing to say.

She told Losman how she'd found Kramer slouched on the stairwell, sleeping. She'd helped him up. "He invited me to his place," she said, "but I said no. He'd wet himself. His pants were stained. I guided him to his apartment, and I cleaned up the mess in the hallway."

"That's very kind of you," Losman said. He watched Caroline chip at the nail of her right index finger, picking at it like she was trying to remove a difficult stain. She was an odd duckling, an artist and filmmaker who, as the bio on her website indicated, also made short promotional films for corporate clients. Losman assumed that was how she earned her living. A single woman a few years younger than Losman, she lived in an *andelslejlighed*—a nearly impossible word to translate because the concept was so foreign to Americans. It was a living arrangement in which you became a member of a cooperative association and, as a member, could live in an apartment owned by the association. She often dressed like a widow at a funeral, wearing long black skirts and boots and painting her face with heavy eyeliner, sometimes smearing a black teardrop down one corner of each eye for effect. Losman was, of course, absolutely smitten by her.

Last summer, he found a flyer taped to the mailboxes in the entrance of their building. It was an advertisement for an exhibition she was giving in the Bohemian freetown of Christiana. When he got there, he found an old three-story villa that had fallen into disrepair like so much of Christiana, and immediately entered a narrow foyer that smelled tartly of fresh paint. He'd expected to see people milling about examining Caroline's artwork, sipping wine from plastic cups like they do at these things, but the only person there was Caroline. She stood stiffly erect in a prim, blue skirt and yellow blouse.

"Thank you for coming," she said, trying to smile.

"Where is everybody?" Losman said and instantly regretted it. He knew from several of his own poorly attended readings the vulnerability you feel when no one comes to your event. When no one cares.

Caroline's face flushed with embarrassment. She pointed to a separate, adjoining room. "The exhibition begins there, if you'd like to see it."

The exhibition space was a wide, airy hall, bright and quiet, tomblike in its stillness. There he saw arrayed a number of artworks on easels. Her dark, morbid drawings were a series of black and white charcoal panels. They depicted, as indicated on a small placard next to Caroline's bio, "the struggles of a teenager named Claudia, an anorexic, depressed, lonely girl hungry to escape the confines of her small-town life and connect with an authentic self."

Was Claudia Caroline's alter ego, or just some haunted figure she'd invented? In one panel, he saw Claudia staring into a mirror in a large room crowded with people; the mirror showed no reflection but for the throng scuttling around her, either ignoring Claudia or not seeing her at all. One of Caroline's films repeated on a constant loop in a small, dark room off the main gallery; it portrayed Claudia as a black and white cubist cartoon figure superimposed on B-roll footage of a bustling, real-life Copenhagen pedestrian street. With her herky-jerky movements, she was decidedly out-of-place in a realist setting. Claudia didn't fit in. And neither did Caroline.

Losman was impressed. He spent nearly an hour studying her art, biding his time and hoping in vain that others would soon arrive. She was a very good artist, he thought, and she deserved the audience that never came.

But *this*—today on the stairwell—was the closest he'd ever been to her, and Losman could feel the high-wire tension in him, his urge to tic. He sublimated this urge by continuously pumping his hand at his side as if he were squeezing an imaginary ball, a blending in trick he'd learned in elementary school after being teased by his classmates.

When it came to his Tourette, Losman was a hider. He didn't want anyone to know. By outward appearance he was a successful, well-adjusted man. He wasn't gregarious or outgoing, like Kat, but he could slot into most conversations without attracting undue attention to himself. When people thought of Tourette Syndrome, they usually thought of the poor souls who involuntarily barked *fuck you! bitch! fat pig!* in public. Coprolalia, that's what that was—and it wasn't that common. But coprolalic fits made for great television and garnered an outsize amount of public attention. Losman's version of Tourette was relatively mild, as these things go, but it was still debilitating. A big downer. Few people would ever guess that, in private, no longer tethered to the leash he kept them on in public, his tics and twitches ran amok on him, as if making up for lost time, or that in a very bleak moment—as a new father who found himself single and alone, his infant son in the care of another man—he once sprawled out face-down on the bathroom floor whimpering to a God he didn't even believe in to please make this nightmare end. Never guess that, as he translated, alone in his room, he jerked his head repeatedly. Sometimes, at night, his twitches were so forceful that he rocked the bed, keeping himself awake. He didn't want to live like this.

He would give *any*thing to lead a tic-free life.

But he couldn't stop ticcing. When he suppressed his tics in public, like at this very moment on the stairwell with Caroline, an uncomfortable tension would grow in his body until he was forced to tic as soon as he was out of eyesight. When he was out in public for extended periods of time, Losman found more discreet ways to release this tension, usually by transferring the tic to his fingers and toes, or blinking once or twice, fiercely. It was like rotating a valve and slowly letting off the steam when too much pressure had built up in the pipes. These tricks worked, and nobody noticed him at his worst. But the act of suppressing his tics took its toll on Losman's mind and body. It was a contradictory, Jekyll-and-Hyde existence—both a façade and a reality. And he felt it now. Felt it hard.

Caroline shifted her feet, and accidentally scraped the sole of her sneaker against the floor, producing that sharp, squeaky sound basketball players make on the court. "He did something else," she said. "I'm embarrassed to even say."

"What?" Losman asked.

She didn't respond right away, and Losman wondered if she'd decided not to tell him. Then she said, glancing up at the railing that overlooked the stairwell, "He unzipped his fly and masturbated right there."

"Ugh," Losman said. He balled and unballed his fist. "That's terrible." The Danish word for terrible, *forfærdeligt*, always sounded pathetic emerging from Losman's mouth, even after fifteen years in Denmark. Like a first grader trying to pronounce a word he didn't understand. But Caroline's thoughts were clearly elsewhere.

"Don't worry," she said. "The super cleaned it up."

"Jesus," he said, in English. Losman felt like an overfilled balloon, stretched past the breaking point, soon to burst. Slowly, carefully, he moved his head from side to side, a half measure of release. It didn't work. But as if the word *cleaned* jogged his brain enough to kick his olfactory nerves into gear, he noticed the strong antiseptic smell in the stairwell, a thick lemony sweetness. On the landing below, a patch of sunlight shone through the window, swabbing his skin in its warmth.

"I felt very badly for him."

"You're not *mad* at him for doing that?" Losman said. He tried to recall his interactions with Kramer. He'd always been eager to escape the man's prattle, his beer and cigarette breath. Sometimes, when Kramer was returning from Aldi with his bottles of beer and Losman was heading out of the building, he would stop him to chat. For some reason he liked Losman. In a slurred Copenhagener accent, whiny and truculent and drunkenly old fashioned, he would say a variation of: *You're an American, you're okay. You're the right kind of foreigner! You speak Danish! You work! You look like us! All these foreigners here, they don't even try to learn Danish! They just milk the system*! Kramer was always tense: a geyser timed to blow. Losman would nod and wonder if he should stand up for Denmark's immigrants.

"No," Caroline said. "I'm not mad. He was just a sick and lonely old man." She reached down and clutched Losman's hand, squeezed it, and he felt a jolt of electricity at her unexpected touch, her warm skin on his. "Do you think he killed himself?" she asked.

He studied the veins in her hands, her long slender fingers, her painted nails. Unable to speak, wondering why she was holding his hand, he cleared his throat softly, blinking hard, just once. The urge to tic was volcanic, a river of hot lava oozing and bubbling beneath the surface. He needed to let it gush out, but not when Caroline was around.

They heard sirens wailing in the distance. When the ambulance arrived, Caroline abruptly let go of his hand and stood. "Well, I'm going home."

"What? Aren't you going to wait?"

"I can't."

Losman watched her scuttle downstairs to her third-floor apartment. Heard her door open, then close, the latch clicking in the lock. As soon as she was gone, he jerked his head repeatedly, like a man having a violent seizure, chuffing air through his mouth as if he had something stuck in his throat. He felt instantly better. When the men rumbled into the building, he got to his feet and hurriedly padded down two flights to his own apartment on the second floor. He closed the door softly and stood listening with his ear planed to the wood. Indistinct chatter. Voices. Clipped words. Broken sentences. The heavy thump of boots clomping past his door. The static of some kind of walkie-talkie. The crew must've had a master key or a locksmith, because within minutes the noise on the landing had abated; the men had made it inside Kramer's apartment.

Losman pushed back from the door and stared at his laptop screen. It had gone dark in his absence, *fallen asleep* was the expression. Propped next to his computer, open to page 186 of 570 pages, was the crime novel he was translating. With his simple method of translating 10 pages a day Losman would, in theory, complete the book in another 38 1/2 days, but he didn't like to work weekends, especially when Aksel was visiting. This was a pretty good system that enabled him to pay rent, buy food, and live modestly by translating books. It wasn't the life he'd imagined for himself, but it was something. He had steady work, a roof over his head, and a wonderful child. All good things.

He lived on Nordre Frihavnsgade in the Østerbro district, a main thoroughfare near The Triangle, a central hub where five avenues met.

He went to the window and stared down at the busy street below. An ambulance and a cherry-red firetruck were parked along the bike path. Cars slowed down as they approached the emergency vehicles, before edging around them and scooting away. A cluster of bicyclists, moving *en masse* like a swarm of bees, buzzed past in a blur of motion. On the sidewalk, a young woman wearing a powder-blue windbreaker was pushing a baby stroller, a man in a smart gray suit walking beside her with a bag from the local bakery in his hand. Directly across from Losman's window was another building. In one of the apartments, one level below, a slim, bald man was tapping at his computer keyboard. Was he writing a novel? Losman wondered. Losman fingered the hasp on the window. He pulled it up, freed it from its hook, and opened his window outward like a small door. Then he fastened the hasp to a knob on the sill and caught a slight breeze. He braced his hands on the sill and leaned out. Would he survive a fall onto the flagstones below? Probably, he thought, he'd just end up a quadriplegic in a wheelchair.

Losman jutted his lower lip and squirted out a puff of air, the latest incarnation of his vocal tics. For as long as he could remember his tics would cycle in and out in an endless, repeating loop. Head jerks, rapid eye blinks, finger waggles, neck rolls, snorts, throat-clearing, small clicking noises. His tics were like unwanted house guests showing up at random intervals, sleeping in his bed, and overstaying their welcome. One would appear, take over, and dominate—only to be replaced a few months later by another.

When he'd moved to Copenhagen, he'd been filled with an expat's giddy optimism. But when Kat left him, her passion for him having run aground on the shoals of what she'd pointedly called his "hopeless passivity," he'd found this place through a mutual friend. Later, he'd discovered that Kat had timed their breakup to coincide with the apartment's vacancy—an act of kindness in a city that was notoriously difficult to find an apartment, especially on this street. Either that or she was assuaging her own guilt and making her life easier knowing that her ex-boyfriend, the father of her child, wouldn't have to live with her until he found a new place, which would have been especially awkward on those occasions when she brought her boyfriend home for the night. The new boyfriend, Losman assumed, was Mr. Actively Hopeful.

But Losman had done very little to give his place the appearance that someone actually lived here. Apart from his books, which he'd stuffed into bookshelves he'd bought at Bilka, there was only a recliner, a couch, a bed, a dining table, and a small desk. No fixtures adorned the walls. No plants cozied up the space. In one corner of the room, he kept a toy-filled play area for Aksel.

Two flights above, he heard the emergency crew's heavy footfalls on the landing, and the babble of their voices. But he couldn't make out what they were saying. Within a minute, the men trundled past his door, and soon they exited the building carrying a stretcher. It was covered with a white sheet. Beneath the white sheet lay the unmistakable form of a human body.

2

AFTER THE EMERGENCY CREW HAD LEFT, Losman tried to work on the translation, but he couldn't focus. He cracked open a beer, drained it quickly, and drank another. He snorted and puffed and jerked his head, once, twice, a third time until he'd temporarily satisfied the urge in his brain. Already he'd wasted four hours that day subjected to the miserable, regurgitated prose of this horrible, no-good heap of rot— Niels H. Petersen's debut novel of insufferable pomposity called *Jeg slår dig ihjel.* The novel was about a gruff old detective named Niels P. who tracks down a serial killer only to discover that the serial killer was his split personality, P. Nielsen. So far, Losman had rendered the title directly as *I Am Going to Kill You.* Since the book was slowly killing Losman, it seemed a fitting title. Somehow, the novel had garnered excellent reviews in fawning Danish newspapers and subsequently sold a bunch of copies to unsuspecting readers. A British publisher, like a pig feeding at the trough, then bought the rights and hired Losman. He would've said no way am I translating this trash, but the money was very good, and he needed it. Petersen had followed up this debut with a novel called *Terror*, a sequel whose premise was even more batshit: after inexplicably avoiding jail time for murdering six women in *I Am Going to Kill You*, Niels P. and P. Nielsen "partner" to track down a serial rapist who terrorizes the city of Aarhus and who turns out, equally inexplicably, to be a radicalized Muslim immigrant. The launch party for this second novel was tonight, and Losman had been invited by the publisher. He'd accepted the invitation because if he wanted to translate other books—and how else was he going to earn a living?—he had to play nice.

As a translator, Losman felt most days like a lowly scribe in some damp, chilly medieval monastery, forced to copy, at great personal cost, every ridiculous page. Laboriously he plodded his way through one sentence after another. His syntax bothered him. The sentences were like a Mr. Potato Head with its parts in all the wrong places. It made him anxious to think that he wouldn't get all his pages done today; it meant he would have to translate fourteen pages tomorrow or four pages on the weekend to catch up, to stay on schedule. But he couldn't concentrate. He pictured Kramer schlumping up the stairs, breathing heavily, beer bottles clinking in his hand. He pictured him on the landing with his lovely young neighbor. He pictured his lonely final hours, and he couldn't help but wonder if Kramer really had killed himself. When his thoughts turned to how desperate a man would have to be to end his own life, Losman backed away from his computer and decided it was time for a mind-cleansing jog.

THE LAKES IN COPENHAGEN are a series of manmade, rectangular reservoirs between Østerbrogade and Gammel Kongevej. A wide trail frames the lakes, and on this mild, sunny day the trail teemed with joggers in fancy running gear, parents pushing expensive strollers, and happy squawking children.

When he was done with his day's work, Losman liked to jog these lakes, circumnavigating their 4-mile perimeter and admiring the grand, five-story apartment complexes that surrounded them. He was in good shape, his body lithe and limber for a 43-year-old man. His sneakers pounded the ground, crunching and popping on the gravel. Unlike others he met on the trail, who needed to fill the void in their head by pumping some kind of beat into it, Losman did not jam earbuds into his ears and blast music. He wanted his mind and body pure when he jogged.

It was April, and the early afternoon sky sparkled; the bright sun cast an inverted triangle across the smooth surface of the water, glinting like crystals of gold. Ducks floated lazily past. Swans preened, congregating near the water's edge, waiting for handouts from passersby. Sharp rods of sunlight banked off the red brick facades of the apartment complexes, giving them a coppery glow. It was a beautiful day, and he felt instantly better for the fresh, cool air circulating in his lungs, air that was clean and redolent of budding spring flowers. The muscles in his calves and thighs churned, working hard to propel him forward. Still, he was out of sync and couldn't find his rhythm, and his breathing was ragged. He was panting like a dog. He couldn't put the episode with Caroline out of his mind. They hardly knew each other. Why would she hold *his* hand, even momentarily?

Was it some kind of signal? Did she secretly find him and his brown eyes attractive? He was six feet tall, trim and fit, with a complement of thick brown hair. With his trendy wire-rimmed glasses, the kind that were popular in Europe but made him look like a snob back home in Philly, he mostly fit in here. But he also knew that if someone were to hold up an encyclopedia photo depicting the average middle-aged white male—a man so plain that you instantly looked right through him, a man who did not make a lasting impression—that photo would resemble him.

So, after some labored deliberations on the matter, Losman came to the inevitable conclusion that she couldn't possibly be interested in him. His physical appearance aside, he was a middling literary translator with Tourette. The truth of the matter was, Caroline had clutched his hand only because they'd seen a dead man together.

He thought of Kramer. What a miserable, sad-sack way to go. No one deserved to die in such an ignoble way, not even a churlish prick like Kramer. What had he been like as a child? A young man? Where and when had his life derailed? Losman knew so very little about him. Had he been married? Did his wife pre-decease him, or did she divorce him? Was that why he was such a bitter drunkard? Did he have children? If so, did they love him or despise him? What about his hopes and dreams? He must've had some once. Did he recall fond memories of his childhood? Dancing around the Christmas tree singing songs while holding his mother's hand? Picking apples with his siblings? Fishing with his father off a pier?

So many questions Losman would never know answers to. He'd shunned Kramer, kept his distance as if the man reeked of skunk, and now he was gone. Losman was ashamed that he'd made no attempt to befriend the old man. Wasn't that the moral of the John Prine song "Hello in There"? To stop and care about others? Sure, he was a racist, immigrant-bashing, reactionary curmudgeon, but he must've had *some* redeeming qualities. Doesn't everyone? Maybe if Losman had talked to him more Kramer wouldn't have been so lonely, and he wouldn't be dead.

Losman rubbed sweat from his forehead and plodded forward. He'd run about two miles now and he just wasn't feeling it, not today. The second beer had been a mistake. He'd kept an even pace, but not a strong one. A dark-haired woman pushing a three-wheeled pram, inside of which a chubby-cheeked baby lay thickly bundled, jogged up on his immediate right. Losman turned to watch her pass. All at once he snorted, piglike, causing the woman to look up, flinching. Losman mumbled a quick apology. But the woman, clearly uneasy, picked up her pace and pulled away from him. If only he could tell her that he couldn't help himself, his Tourette was a fucking nightmare to live with.

He watched the woman's back gaining distance, racing away from him as if he were some kind of freak, and he halted abruptly, unable to continue. In that moment, it occurred to him that *he* was Kramer: a hermit who drank too much, who'd become set in his ways like an old man. Losman had many acquaintances, most of them related to his work, but he had few friends. Danes were notoriously difficult to get close to, and this was certainly true for him. There once was an eclectic group of expatriates he hung out with, guys from around the globe who'd been in the same cohort at the Danish language school, who'd bonded over their common failure to utter the phrase *rødgrød med flød* without sounding like bullfrogs trying to vocalize human speech. They hailed from Spain, Ecuador, South Africa, Ukraine, New Zealand, Kenya, Great Britain, Ireland, Canada, Israel, and Italy, and for a time they were quite the exotic bunch. But as the years went by, the group slowly diminished, dissolving like antacid in water. Some went back home after their relationships foundered, others started families and moved to the safety and monotony of the suburbs. Since splitting up with Kat, he hadn't invited a single one of these guys to his new place. No particular reason for it, he just didn't want to. His only real visitor was his son. And no matter how much joy Aksel brought him, the kid was only three and couldn't bear the burden of being his father's only friend. *You're a sad excuse for a man*, Losman thought.

Feeling low, he stood in place for a minute, gazing at a flock of ducks swimming past him on the water. Then he turned and began the slow walk home, snorting and squeezing his hand into a ball. He'd barely got his pulse up today, and now he was dejected. No, not dejected. Defeated was the better word. How could a man work so hard and have so little to show for it? Sure, he had books with his name on them, but so what? At the end of each month, following expenses, he was left with around four thousand Danish kroner in his bank account, a pittance, and his retirement fund back in the U.S. was stalled—last time he checked—at $9,500 and change. He glanced at his watch. A couple minutes past 4:00 p.m. From here it would take him a solid 40 minutes to walk home, leaving him with little time to shower, eat, and catch the bus downtown to tonight's event.

As a child, Losman had read one of those thin, syrupy biographies of George Washington written for kids. In it he'd found an off-hand passage, what the author had clearly intended as a minor detail, about

Washington's fear of being buried alive. How he'd wanted his body laid out for three full days to prove he was dead. Losman had dwelled on this detail for days, and Washington's fear became his. And for a while it consumed his waking thoughts; he imagined what it would be like to wake up in a sealed coffin underground, abandoned, unable to escape, your screams muffled by six feet of dirt. Although Losman was no longer afraid of being buried alive, what as an adult he'd learned was called taphephobia, the fear of being alone in dark, enclosed spaces remained to this day. And at this moment he felt a rush like vertigo, flipping his world inside out. His fear had become reality: He *was* alone, he *was* abandoned. The only difference was that he found himself in a vast space bright with daylight.

A girl shrieked, followed by a woman shouting *Nej! Nej!* And Losman looked up just in time to see a swan, perched on the edge of the lake, flap its wings once and violently nip its long orange beak at the little girl, who'd proffered it a hunk of bread. The girl's arm was still outstretched, her hand now empty, as if she didn't know what to do with it. The swan squawked once then lunged at the girl, pouncing on her and battering her with its wings.

Losman acted on impulse, rushing forward and tackling the bird. It was a big swan, soft and fat as a Thanksgiving turkey, and for a brief moment his arms clutched its plump, feathered body as though it were a fluffy pillow. He skidded forward, the bird screeching underneath him. In the next instant, Losman somehow found himself on his back with the bird on top of him, pecking at him with its beak and hammering him with its wings. Losman clenched his right fist and punched the bird; its head was knobbed and bony, yet also smooth and slick, and his blow slipped off. The swan reared back, squawking. It leaped forward and kicked Losman's chest with its little webbed feet. Losman pushed the bird off and stumbled to his knees. A crowd stood watching. Someone grabbed the back of his shirt and helped him up. The swan waddled forward and Losman kicked it in the face. The bird squawked again, one terse quack that in the swan's language probably meant *fuck you, you fucking piece of shit*, and then it waddled back to the reservoir and hopped into the water.

Losman panted, his hands shaky. He watched the swan paddle away, until he felt a hand on his shoulder. *Tusind tak*, the little girl's mother said.

Losman looked at her. She stood with her mouth open, her eyes wide, an expression of horror on her face. Understandable. If a swan ever attacked Aksel, he'd be horror-struck too. The woman held his gaze with such fierce and friendly determination that he was forced to turn away, unaccustomed as he was to someone actually *seeing* him. "Nothing to it," he said, in Danish. *Det var så lidt.* He shook her hand because she offered hers. Then he squatted down next to the little girl, who was crying, and patted her shoulder. "It's okay. You're all right."

The girl squeezed her mother's leg and pressed herself against her thigh. She was so fair skinned and white-haired that she seemed transparent, a ghost girl. Pigtails poked out of either side of her head, choked with slender pink ribbons.

"*Undskyld*," the girl spluttered through her tears.

"Why are *you* sorry?" Losman said.

The girl's mother squatted. "Eva," she said. "You did nothing wrong."

Losman leaned forward and whispered to the girl, "Do you know what that bird was?"

The girl turned to her mother, as if to check whether it was okay for her to talk to this man, this stranger. Her mother smiled, then nodded for Losman to continue.

"A big dumb idiot!"

The girl's face brightened, and she laughed.

"My son is three," Losman said. "How old are you?"

She held up three fingers before squinching her face in concentration and adding a fourth.

"*Four!*" he said, playful. "I bet you'll remember this day when you're my age. But don't let that mean old swan get to you. Not all swans are such big dumb idiots. And some started out as ugly ducklings, remember."

WHEN HE RETURNED TO HIS APARTMENT, Losman was pleased to find a plate of brownies on his doormat, with a thank you note from Caroline. *Tusind tak*, it read. *Tak fordi du var der. Det kunne jeg ikke har klaret uden dig.* He set the plate on his table, pulled back the plastic wrap, and ate a chewy square; it was a tasty treat, gooey with dark chocolate, and Losman devoured it in two mouthfuls. He removed his shirt and stared at the fist-sized bruise that had bloomed on his right shoulder, the result of his confrontation with the swan. With two fingers he pressed it like a button, and he felt a tender, delicious prickle of pain. He opened the tap and gulped a slug of water, catlike, his head under the faucet, before taking a brief, unsatisfactory shower in his tiny corner stall. After pulling on a pair of clean jeans and a button-down cotton shirt, he brushed his teeth. As he scraped the hard bristles across his teeth, he jerked his head three or four times, hard, and in the process, he spattered his cotton shirt with toothpaste and left a foamy pink stain on his breast pocket. *Fuck, fuck*, he said, and changed his shirt.

On his way out, Losman locked his door and stood for a moment on the landing, listening. It was an old building, and it was not uncommon to hear a toilet flush or voices spirited across rooms through the thin walls. But on this day, at this pre-dinner hour, all was quiet, so he tromped down the stairs and thrust open the door into the waxy cool light of late afternoon. Turning right, he spotted his bus slowly grinding its way through bumper-to-bumper traffic, and he darted across the street.

Standing among the gathered throng at the bus stop, he glanced up at his own building and was startled by the sight of Caroline at her third story window. She was no longer wearing her cloche hat and gabardine coat but a bright pink, full-length kimono decorated with white flowers and belted with a thin yellow sash, an *obi*. He'd once translated a Norwegian historical novel set in Japan, an experience that represented the paltry sum of his knowledge of Japanese culture; the author had transformed an *obi* into a ham-handed symbol, so it was easy to remember it now. Caroline had pulled her hair up, too, in what he assumed was a traditional Japanese bun, with what appeared to be chopsticks run through like scaffolding holding it all together: she was pretending to be a geisha, he guessed, a pale, blonde Nordic variety with bright blue eyes and small red lips. He turned and followed her line of vision until he saw what she was staring at: a bare lightbulb glowing like a tiny sun in an apartment across the street. Sunlight cut slantwise, splitting the street in two, bathing one half (his current side) into shade and the other half (where Caroline stood) in light. What was in that apartment? he wondered. From his vantage point, all he could see was the bare lightbulb.

By the time Losman turned back to Caroline, she was gone. He shoved his hands in the pockets of his windbreaker and watched the bus approach. Brakes squealed. Horns pipped. There was a low frequency of noise, a city hum, a congestion of voices. The streets were thick with rush-hour traffic, mostly people heading out of the city to the suburbs—Ballerup, Hillerød, Hvidovre, Vanløse, Lyngby—and knots of bicyclists gliding by.

A hot gust of fumes warmed his face when the bus arrived. Losman covered his mouth and nose and waited for passengers to stumble out. The bus was crowded, and rather than sit, he grabbed hold of a pole and stood for the entire ten-minute ride down Dag Hammerskjold's Avenue to Østerport station.

Fifteen years ago, an American transplant, abroad for the first time in his life, he was held in thrall by everything he saw in Copenhagen. He'd grown up near Philadelphia, with its old red brick rowhouses and cobblestone primness, and yet the unfamiliarness of this city made him feel delightfully off-kilter. Its tight downtown was rich with color, a palimpsest of more than 800 years of architectural styles and history.

In the first few months after moving to Copenhagen, as Kat started her job with the magazine *Kvinde*—where she would later work her way up to Art Director—Losman took his language classes and explored the city: the bakeries, the shops, the sidewalk cafes, bookstores, and small neighborhood groceries, the long blocks of sturdy brick apartment complexes. But it was the language, especially the language, that drew him in like a bee to nectar: the dips and curves and glottal stops. He remembered standing on a train platform once as a woman spoke three magical words into a loudspeaker: *Struer over Aarhus*. Destinations unknown to him then. The language sounded warbly, birdlike, the words dropping low and shooting back up. Once, while driving with Kat through the forests of her home region in North Zealand one cold winter morning, he'd listened to the news on the radio and thought: I will never learn this language. There was a blanket of crisp white frost on the ground, and low hills merged with dense clusters of birch and elm and pine. Pleased and contented, he sat back and closed his eyes, allowing the trilling voice of the newscaster to fill his ears, then reached out and laid his hand on Kat's knee.

But now, all that was stripped away. He stared out the window as pedestrians trudged on the sidewalk, hands in pockets, eyes downcast or mesmerized by the luminous glare of the cell phones they held cupped in their palms like baby birds. With the exception of the occasional café or restaurant, the stores they passed were exactly like the ones he'd find back home in Philly: Subway, McDonald's, Burger King, 7-Eleven, Apple. Globalization's heavy footprint left an unsubtle mark. He'd lived in Copenhagen for so long that it seemed plain to him now, a kind of Everycity filled with Everypeople. And in some sense, he didn't see it now, either. It was home, and home was something you took for granted.

AFTER LEAVING THE STATION, he had a five-minute walk to the publisher's, taking him past Tivoli and City Hall. As he went, Losman felt increasingly jittery. Nervous sweat formed on his forehead, and he swiped it away with the back of his hand. He chuffed air through his nose, cleared his throat repeatedly, and jerked his head from side to side. Anxiety worsened his tics. More than anything, he dreaded his arrival, that awkward and terrible moment when people paused their conversations to look up at him, only to quickly turn away, disinterested. To quell this anxiety, he made a slight detour and stopped at a nondescript Irish pub and ordered a Carlsberg, which he drank quickly, without pleasure, while standing at the bar as Frank Sinatra's "My Way" blared from the corner speakers.

The bar was three blocks from the publisher's office. He downed his beer, paid, and left. Out on the street, he passed a construction site gone silent for the day. He paused to peer behind the long wooden wall that had been built as a temporary barrier. What he saw was a massive gaping hole twenty to thirty feet deep where a building used to stand and where another would soon be erected; parked in the hole were several large yellow digging machines with enormous wheels. Losman made a mental note to bring Aksel here soon—the boy loved machinery—before sauntering on. Since he was in no hurry to get to the book launch, he inspected the posters and flyers people had tacked on the makeshift barrier: concerts, poetry readings, theatre openings, art installations, babysitting and dog-walking services, English and German-language tutors. The usual.

Then he spotted a sheet of plain white A4 paper, an advertisement for a company he'd never heard of, FuturePerfect Laboratories. It was written in Danish with an accompanying English translation, which Losman found clumsy. One of the hazards of his work was that he was constantly judging the translations he found in museums, restaurants, train stations, etc. He couldn't help himself.

"Do you struggle with addiction? Anxiety? Depression? Do you have ADHD, ADD, Tourette syndrome, or similar? Do you want answers? If you answer yes to these questions and wish to participate in memory therapy, call the number listed below."

What the *hell*? Losman thought. He glanced to his left and right as if he might find the person who'd tacked this poster on the wall. No one paid him any mind. His eyes slid back to the advertisement and scrolled to the bottom of the page, to the tear sheets that lined the paper like a row of large, jagged teeth. Two rectangles had already been ripped off. He braced his left hand against the flyer and, with his right, yanked off a tooth and carefully stuffed it in his pocket.

WHEN LOSMAN ARRIVED AT THE LAUNCH, the party was already in full swing. In the foyer, a young woman he didn't recognize—one of the many interns the publisher cycled through—welcomed him with a bright, gap-toothed smile. She wore a dark-blue blouse fringed at the hem and huge red eyeglasses much too large for her narrow face. She checked his name off a list and handed him a glossy bookmark. Losman held it in his hand, staring at Niels H. Petersen's handsome, stylishly grizzled visage, which was austere and contemplative, like an actor playing the role of serious artiste. Politely he slipped the bookmark into his pocket.

He pushed his way through the tight murmuring crowd, heading straight for the bar. No one gave him a second glance. The bartender handed him a bottle of Carlsberg wrapped in a damp white cocktail napkin. He took a long pull and was glad to have something in his hand. Ariadne Books was located on Studiestræde near Bispetorvet and Vor Frue Kirke, in a majestic three-story brick building from the 1830s, once the private home of a shipping magnate. The party was being held in the spacious loft; the roof was pitched at a steep angle, an upside-down V, and original beams—thick as pillars—crisscrossed the room. Heavy oak shelves larded with Ariadne's fifty-year history of publishing lined the walls; the books were just decoration here, *pynt* was the snappy Danish word for it. The wooden floor had been buffed for the occasion; it was smooth and clean, shiny as a bald man's dome. In the center of the room was an island studded with plates of finger foods, but smartly dressed servers carried trays among the guests. Through one window, Losman could see the peak of the terracotta roof of the neighboring building and, beyond that, the terracotta roof-scape of the entire city, the ubiquitous network of windmills seeming to float out on Øresund, and even a thin sliver of Sweden.

He spotted a fellow American translator with whom he was friendly chatting up a renowned female poet. He started in that direction but swerved away when he realized that the pair were locked in intimate conversation—like lovers meeting on the sly. In turning away, he bumped into Lars Andreasson, Ariadne's Swedish publisher. Andreasson was a tall man with a head of thick silver hair. He squeezed Losman's shoulder and greeted him with false enthusiasm.

"Losman!" he said. "Glad you could make it. How is the translation coming along?"

Andreasson's Swedish always confounded Losman. The warbly birdlike dips that he was accustomed to in Danish seemed steeper in Swedish, like descending over perilous rocky cliffs with only one wing. It took him a moment to find his balance.

"Fine," he said, tilting his head back to look up at Andreasson. "Thirty-eight and a half more days until I have the first draft done."

"Why the half?"

"I had a slight complication today."

Andreasson nodded but, to Losman's relief, didn't inquire into the nature of the complication. His watery-blue eyes wandered the room, as if searching for somewhere he could escape to. "What do you think of *Terror*? Wonderful, isn't it? Better than the first book?"

Losman felt a powerful urge to jerk his head, but he managed to settle it by clearing his throat. He eyed the poet and the translator as the poet laid her hand gently on the translator's elbow, and he was stabbed with a vague sensation of jealousy. The poet was known for her hyper-sexualized verse, and the translator was the lucky dog who got to recreate it in English—did he get to *experience* it, too? He turned his attention back to Andreasson. "It'll sell for sure," he said. "It's a perfect novel for today's marketplace."

"Exactly! I trust you're capturing Petersen's unique voice in *I Am Going to Kill You*? It's that voice that really makes the book special."

Losman drank his beer, wondering which part of Petersen's voice Andreasson thought was unique. The heavy reliance on trite police procedural clichés? The wooden dialogue packed with clotted chunks of exposition that no human would ever say in conversation? "Sure, I've got it down."

"Good, good," Andreasson said. He glanced openly around the room now, head pivoting like an owl's. He squeezed Losman's shoulder again. "Well, I'm going to mingle."

Losman exhaled in relief, watching Andreasson merge into a conversation that included Petersen and a small, bespectacled man he recognized as an important literary critic, one of those highbrow types who liked to sprinkle English, French, and German phrases into his reviews. He finished his beer and went for another. As he waited in line, a German translator appeared at Losman's side. Rüdiger Steinbach.

"Hello, Rudy," he said.

"Hello, Daniel."

Losman was grateful for Rudy's presence now, even though he was, quite possibly, even more awkward than Losman. He was the type of person who might suddenly appear in the middle of a conversation, attentive but mute, like a creepy kid brother you don't want around. After Losman got his beer, he joined Rudy in sputtered conversation along the rear wall, away from others. Rudy, he discovered, was the translator responsible for bringing *I Am Going to Kill You* into German.

Having little to say to one another, they made small talk about translation theory—a subject that didn't interest Losman at all. But Rudy was a nerd about it, and he was heated up by a recent article he'd read in *The Guardian*. Losman watched Rudy's thin lips move, and he nodded at the appropriate moments. But before long he grew bored, and the tension in his body became as taut as a guide wire; to satisfy his urge to tic, he cleared his throat discreetly and balled his right hand into a fist, then stretched his fingers several times until he felt okay. He had the sense that he and Rudy could remain in this very spot for the rest of the party, and no one would know or even care. He needed to get away from Rudy. There was a balcony on the other side of the room. From where he stood, he could see bright tufts of clouds like fat Styrofoam peanuts glowing orange on the horizon. He longed to be out there, away from others, and watch the sun set.

"I'm going to get another beer," he told Rudy, patting his shoulder.

He slipped through the crowd. He got the beer and made his way to the balcony. The night was cool and Losman felt a great, heady relief at finally being alone. He moved away from the door so that he was out of sight, pulled up a chair, and sat down, his back against the building. He jerked his head a few times to clear his mind, before taking a long, satisfying pull from his beer.

The bruise on his shoulder had stiffened. Gently he prodded it with his fingers, and in doing so, felt the bookmark he'd stuffed in his pocket. Losman pincered it between his fingers and pulled it out, along with the slip of paper he'd torn from the advertisement. He stared at Petersen's mug. It didn't seem fair that such a poser could be feted on such a grand scale, could have not one but two novels to his name. All he'd done was copy the formula Dan Brown had so successfully mastered: short cliffhanger chapters, manic plot twists, sudden and jarring shifts in time and place. Reading one of his books was more like watching some made-for-television action movie with 30-second sequences stitched into some slapdash pattern that eventually formed a narrative. He stood up and leaned over the railing. He held the bookmark out and let it fall, watching with satisfaction as the small glossy slip of paper twisted and turned in the air like a leaf.

Then he turned his attention to the advertisement. What kind of therapy were they offering? Over the years, to combat his tics, he'd been to behavioral therapy sessions. And though he'd refused to take any of the antipsychotic drugs, like risperidone, doctors sometimes prescribed for Tourette for fear of what it would do to his body and mind, he had taken one hypertension drug called guanfacine that was supposed to help. Instead, he'd wake up parched and miserable in the middle of the night. He'd even practiced meditation and yoga and smoked pot. Nothing had ever helped, and he had no reason to believe that some new therapy might drive the curse away. Still, Losman was curious, especially since the randomness of finding the advertisement didn't feel random at all, it felt like something bigger. Like something cosmic. Did he believe in cosmic occurrences? No, he did not. But he pulled his cell phone out anyway and opened his email. Because why the hell not? He pressed compose, typed in the email address for the memory study, and quickly tapped a brief message in Danish: *I have Tourette Syndrome,* he wrote, *and I am interested in participating in your study. Thank you.*

He hit send. Just as the message whooshed away, there was a scuffling noise behind him. Turning, he saw Niels H. Petersen of all people emerging onto the balcony, followed closely by the intern with oversized red eyeglasses who'd handed him the very bookmark he'd just tossed over the railing.

"Losman!" Petersen said. "Jeg har kigget efter dig!"

Losman cleared his throat. In Danish he said, "Well, you found me."

"What are you doing out here? My party's in there, y' know?"

"Needed some air."

"Air? Looks like you need another *beer.*" Petersen gestured at the nearly empty bottle in Losman's hand. He turned to the young woman beside him, who gazed up at him with the wide-eyed admiration of a girl meeting a famous actor, her childhood crush. No woman had ever looked at Losman like that, not even Kat; she was starstruck or maybe in love, probably both. And why wouldn't she be? The asshole was successful *and* handsome. He was wearing black from head to toe: shiny patent-leather shoes, trousers, and a suit jacket that looked like it cost more money than Losman was even making to translate his ridiculous book. Beneath the jacket he wore, of all things, a black turtleneck. Like in his author photo, he kept a fashionable layer of stubble on his cheeks, and his wavy, dirty-blond hair was pinned up in a thick man-bun.

"Be a good girl, Janne," Petersen said, cupping the intern's cheeks and planting a light kiss on her forehead, "and fetch us two Carlsbergs."

The intern nodded eagerly before hustling back to the party for the beers. Petersen watched her go. "What d'ya think, Losman? Pretty girl?" Petersen had one of those devious smiles that was all teeth, what Stephen King would call a shit-eating grin.

"Sure," Losman said. "I guess."

Like a yoga instructor preparing for a session, Petersen closed his eyes, sucked a deep breath, and rolled his head from side to side. "I'd like to see some pages," he said.

"What do you mean?"

"I mean pages. From my book. The one you're translating?"

Losman winced. He didn't like the idea of Petersen reading his translation, not yet. A translator friend of his had once let her famous Spanish author see her work-in-progress, and he'd screamed bloody murder and got her fired from the book; the publisher had forced her to pay back her advance, and no publisher would touch her now. He tilted his head back and drained his beer. If Petersen enlisted Lars Andreasson in his cause, Losman knew, he might campaign the English publisher to force him to show Petersen the pages, and if that happened now, the manuscript was far from ready and Losman could suffer the same fate as his friend. Maybe he'd be replaced by some AI program that would make him permanently obsolete. He balled and unballed his fist to contain the pressure in his head.

Niels noticed. "Do you want to punch me, Losman?"

"What?" Losman said, confused. "No."

Niels lifted his chin and tapped it with a finger. "Go ahead, man, give me your best shot. Right here."

"I don't want to punch you, Niels. Jesus. Look," he said, "it's the first *draft*. It's way too soon for you to see anything."

"When then?"

"I need a least three months to shine it up."

"Three *months*?" Petersen smirked. "I wrote the entire fucking novel in three months."

Losman cleared his throat and lifted his shoulder to ease the tension in his head, careful not to ball his fist again. "I always do four drafts," he said.

"Four drafts! Why do you need…?" Petersen fell silent. He lowered his eyes to study the bottle in his hand and began chipping at the label with his fingernail. His shoulders sagged, and he seemed to wither, like a balloon losing air. "You don't like it, do you?"

"What? No, it's—" Losman said. Some kind of dark cloud had settled over Petersen, he realized. Was he actually filled with *doubt* below that shiny beautiful exterior? He'd always powered forward like a speeding bullet, heedless of the damage he inflicted on others. Maybe he was like a boy who needed constant praise, vulnerable to criticism because he'd never been criticized. But as tempting as it was to tell Petersen the truth, Losman knew he couldn't speak his mind freely, because that would only get him into trouble when this moment of doubt passed. "It's fine, Niels," he lied.

"I don't believe you," Petersen said, deflated.

"It's fine, Niels. Really." Losman nearly laughed at the absurdity of his stroking Petersen's ego. "I just need to make sure my translation is in good shape, okay?"

The door to the balcony opened and out stepped Janne with a Carlsberg in each fist. She smiled at Petersen, who took the beers from

her with a wink. He turned and handed one of the bottles to Losman.
He said, "I don't think I can wait three months, Losman."

LOSMAN WAS BACK AT HIS COMPUTER THE NEXT MORNING, an invisible Niels H. Petersen now staring over his shoulder. *I want to see those pages, Losman!* Since he had an 11:00 o'clock appointment with his therapist, he plowed through fourteen pages and ended his work by 10:15.

Before leaving his computer, he checked his email and saw a message from pelin.akyurek@futureperfect.dk. RE: hukommelseterapi. The email contained a link to a survey. He clicked on the link and was surprised to find that not a single question had anything to do with memory. Instead he was asked to identify his sex, age, race, marital status, ethnicity, his parents' socioeconomic status, his socioeconomic status, and whether he'd endured any lasting hardships in his life. He hesitated only a moment before he tapped the submit survey button.

He got dressed and trudged down to the musty basement where he kept his bicycle in storage. He hauled it outside, clicked on his helmet, and eased into the bike lane on Nordre Frihavnsgade. The sharp sunlight warmed him, while the cool breeze glided up his arms, neck, and face. The sky was a wide, cloudless panel of blue. The cherry blossoms were lush pink blooms, and the air was sweetened with an aroma of fresh boxwood. He felt good, alive. In Philly, riding your bicycle across town was an extreme sport; you put your life in danger any time you climbed on the saddle. But in Copenhagen, where drivers were accustomed to the flocks of bicycles circling the city like migratory birds, you could follow the slow-chugging train of your thoughts down labyrinthine tunnels and into subconscious warrens without fear of finding your face planted against the hood of an SUV.

Losman pedaled down Nordre Frihavnsgade to Blegdamsvej, passing the Niels Bohr Institute, then took a left onto Fredensgade. On Sortedam Dossering the lakes shimmered like a blade under the bright orange sun. With the warm weather finally here, it seemed that every resident of Copenhagen was out and about.

Marlene Tanner's office was on Nørrebrogade directly opposite the leafy, forest-like Assistens Kirkegård, the final resting place of two of Denmark's legendary scribes, Søren Kierkegaard and Hans Christian Andersen. Her spacious, well-lit apartment—which she shared with her partner, a woman named Anne Sofie—was on the second floor of an 18th-century Rococo building. It had high ceilings, tall windows, and mid-century modern decor. Their sessions took place in the couple's small book-filled office off the dining room.

Marlene was dressed casually in blue jeans, a black turtleneck sweater, and thong sandals that clapped against the tiled floor of her kitchen as she prepared tea. Suffusing the air was the sweet scent of fruits and vegetables that lined baskets dangling from hooks in the ceiling: bananas, oranges, mandarins, plums, apples, grapes, potatoes, yams, and other tubers he didn't know the names of; on the counter were jars of granola, mixed nuts, coffee, and spices. Marlene pulled a ginger root from her shiny coffin of a fridge, carved off the skin, and hacked it into thin slices, plunging her knife through the root until it clacked against the wooden cutting board. Chop, chop.

"I'll bring your cup," she said.

He settled into his customary plush chair next to the big window overlooking the cemetery's tall trees. Thick clouds drifted slowly across the sky. The traffic on Nørrebrogade was heavy. While he waited, he pulled out his phone and checked his email. There was already a response from the survey he'd submitted. This Pelin Akyürek was inviting him to meet her and a colleague for a preliminary discussion at a shawarma restaurant downtown. She gave him three date/time options, including one that very evening. But since Aksel was spending the weekend with him, Losman picked the Monday slot and hit send.

A cone of incense burned on a miniature Buddha figurine propped on one of the bookshelves, thin spirals of smoke curling from its orange cherry like from a tiny campfire.

"So, what would you like to discuss today?" Marlene said, handing him his cup of tea. She sat with her iPad in the chair opposite him.

This was her staple question before each session, and Losman was prepared for it. He'd considered telling Marlene all about Kramer, but the more he thought about what he'd say, the more it seemed that Kramer was a diversion from the real subject—*him*. A splash of warm sunshine fell through the open window, and a light breeze carried the aroma of fresh-cut grass from the cemetery. Until a month ago, he'd never visited a psychologist—shrink, head doctor, whatever you wanted to call her—and he was still adjusting to the fact that he was supposed to talk about himself for an entire hour. He liked Marlene, though. She was a silver-haired Canadian from suburban Toronto, probably in her mid-sixties. With her kind, encouraging remarks and her apparent inability to raise her voice, she reminded him of his mother; she wore bifocals attached to a red string like a great aunt or a school librarian, and she was constantly putting them on her nose or letting them sink to her chest. Losman liked these visits because he could speak English to Marlene, the language he felt most whole in. Marlene was a recent transplant to the country, having met her partner only three years before, and she spoke broken Danish. With Marlene, Losman felt as if he were a gobbledygook language to be parsed and interpreted and translated, and this familiarity put him at ease. He always felt rejuvenated following these sessions.

"I signed up for a study," he said. Steam spiraled from his cup and dampened his face. He lifted the tea bag from the now honey-colored water and set it on a little saucer beside him.

"What kind of study?"

"I'm not entirely sure," he said. "It's a memory study."

Marlene removed her eyeglasses and lowered them to her chest. She fixed her brown eyes on him. "Why?" she said. "What made you sign up?"

"I found an ad." Losman jerked his head and snorted. "I suppose technically I'm not part of the study yet. I'll be meeting the facilitators on Monday—at a shawarma bar of all places."

"A shawarma bar? That seems like an odd place to meet."

Losman admitted that it did. He sipped his tea.

"Well, you'll have to tell me how it goes," Marlene said, peering over the rim of her spectacles. "Last time you mentioned how much difficulty you have making new friends because of your Tourette, but we never got into your childhood, and I'd like to know more about the connection between Tourette and your relationships. Do you recall your earliest memory of having Tourette?"

"My earliest memory?" Losman set his teacup down. He cleared his throat and blinked hard, once. "I'm not actually sure when my tics began. What I *remember* is when I started to hide them from others."

"Okay," Marlene said. She lifted her glasses to her nose. "Please elaborate. What we hide from others is always significant. This seems like a good point of entry."

Losman cleared his throat again, this time balling his fist in accompaniment. He steeled himself to share with another person one of his most punishing memories. Only Kat and his mom had heard this story.

"It started in Mrs. Graham's fourth-grade music class," Losman said. He was uncertain where to go next and shifted in his seat. Feeling a low-level strain, he jerked his head once and stared out the window at the tall fir trees lining the cemetery entrance like guardians. How should he tell Marlene this memory? Which details were most important? Finally, he found a thread and stretched it out as far as he could.

"By then I was ticcing a lot. The tics were just part of my life, I didn't think much about them."

"How do you know you were ticcing a lot?" Marlene asked. "Do you remember?"

Losman shook his head. "My mom told me."

"She remembers?"

"She says she does."

Marlene tapped a note into her iPad. "Go on," she said.

Losman frowned, imagining just what Marlene was writing down—*subject relying on someone else's memory to fill the blanks in his own.* He took a deep breath and went on. "Occasionally, one of my classmates would mimic me whenever I blinked my eyes or jerked my head or snorted. Kids laughed. But I was pretty good at shrugging that stuff off."

Marlene fingered her glasses, adjusting them on her nose. "How do you know you were 'pretty good at shrugging that stuff off'?" she asked.

He paused to consider the question, circling back to his childhood, trying to locate any kind of memory to help validate his interpretation of events. But he found nothing, only empty space. A black hole that sucked up everything. "I guess I'm really not sure how," he said.

"Then why do you think you say it?"

"Maybe I want to believe I was?"

"Inventing memories, in other words."

Marlene was right, he knew, it *was* another invention. Why *did* he say it? Was it true? Was he good at shrugging off the laughter? Or was he only pretending to himself that he wasn't affected by it? To picture the scene in his memory, to recall it from wherever it was stored in his brain, he closed his eyes.

The episode with Mrs. Graham had altered his perspective forever. The class was gathered around her in a loose semi-circle, three rows deep; he was in the front row, and they were listening to the Beatles'

"When I'm Sixty-four." Although Mrs. Graham was probably only in her forties, her dark hair was streaked with loops of gray and she seemed much older. About the lesson, or even who was in the classroom with him, Losman recalled very little; in his memory, his classmates were vague blotches. All he pictured was himself and Mrs. Graham, a thickset woman who spoke animatedly with her hands. She loved music, and clearly wanted her charges to love it, too. Midway through the class she leaned forward, and she looked directly at Losman. "Stop," she said. The music kept playing. *Will you still need me, will you still feed me, when I'm sixty-four?*

"What?" he said, confused.

She clicked off the music, then demonstrated what Losman was doing for the entire class to see, jerking her head dramatically. "Stop doing that."

"I can't," he mumbled.

"Yes, you can. And you will."

Losman was embarrassed. Here he was, a little boy sitting in a classroom filled with twenty to twenty-five kids, singled out for public display, shamed by an adult in a position of authority. It felt as though she'd just put a dunce cap on his head and forced him to stand in the corner. In response, Losman lowered his head, humiliated; his classmates' eyes were riveted on him, wondering how he'd respond. *I won't cry*, he told himself, *I won't cry*—his father had once told him that Indians never cried and so neither should he—and so Losman did something he was very good at: he dove inward to a safe place. He stopped listening to the teacher, the music, the others. But the feeling within him, the drive, the irrepressible *need* to shake his head grew steadily, like it always did, tautened like a bow string ready to snap, until, on any other day, at any other moment, he would've shaken his head and released the tension. But not this time. This time he stifled the need. A minute went by following Mrs. Graham's command, then five minutes, but when the next wave of need came, bringing with it that familiar urge to shake his head, Losman squeezed his eyelids shut and willed himself not to give in, not to give in, not to give in. It wasn't easy to fight off this urge, he realized now that he was actually trying. Because his tics have a life of their own, as if an alien creature had invaded his body, he found that suppressing them caused actual physical discomfort. A full-body torment. It was all he could think about, this discomfort, but it was better than being singled out again.

From that day forward, his classmates teased him mercilessly, calling him Blinky and Twitchy, and they impersonated him to gales of laughter; it was as if Mrs. Graham had given them permission to be the cruelest of little fuckers. Losman was grateful for the end of the school year when it came, and he spent the summer learning how to control his tics.

"That was the summer I invented Raffner's Disease," he told Marlene.

"Raffner's Disease?" she said. "What is that?"

"My imagined condition. I pretended I had a non-life-threatening growth in my brain that caused me to twitch. A German by the name of Dr. Heinrich Raffner discovered it. Once my classmates learned I had this growth, I fantasized, they would feel bad for me. They would like me."

"But it was all pretend? Even this Dr. Raffner?"

"Yes. All of it."

"Did you ever tell anyone you had Raffner's Disease?"

"No."

"Okay," Marlene said. "Let's put a pin in that. For now, let's go back to the classroom scene you just described. How did you feel when this happened?"

Losman rubbed his temples. He said, "Well, to be honest, this is where I can't help but wonder if my memory is true. I mean, did it *really* happen the way I remember it? Could Mrs. Graham have been so tactless? Or is my memory so fixated on the humiliation I'd felt that

I invented a scene in a classroom filled with kids all gawping at me like I was a freak?"

"Do you believe you invented this scene, Losman?"

"No," he said. "I mean, not entirely. She definitely told me to stop jerking my head. I will never forget the way she mimicked my head jerks. It was hurtful. But what if she pulled me aside to do so?"

"But the kids teased you afterward, you say?"

"Yeah, but they might've done that anyway. My kid brain might've drawn false connections that I've carried into adulthood. Like a crossword puzzle that I put together wrong. The letters fit in all the squares, but they're not the right letters—or maybe some of them are—and they throw everything off."

Marlene tapped a note on her iPad.

Losman's throat was dry, so he took another slug of tea. He was a grown man far removed from that day in Mrs. Graham's music room, but not a single day had passed since that he hadn't quelled the urge to shake, blink, twitch, sniffle, grunt, or any of the other myriad forms his Tourette took. And telling Marlene about this experience made him feel, what, normal? Heard? Not alone?

"That's why I'm interested in this study," he told Marlene, and cleared his throat. "I feel all mixed up. Maybe I can tear the puzzle apart and put it back together again, correctly?"

THAT AFTERNOON, Kat brought Aksel to the apartment for the weekend. She'd carried him all the way up the stairs, and now he squirmed in her arms. She set him down, and he shambled over to Losman for a high five.

"Hey, buddy," he said.

Aksel lifted one of his Thomas the Train figures up to Losman. "Leger vi med toget?"

"Sure, I'll play trains with you," Losman said cheerily, in English. He always spoke in English to his son, even if the boy refused to speak it to him. He pointed at the plastic IKEA box filled with the wooden train tracks they would assemble for the one millionth time. "After I'm done talking to your mom, okay?"

"Mor har købt den til mig," Aksel said, indicating the train he held in his hand.

"Mama bought that for you? That's great."

Aksel trundled off to his play corner and began to rummage through his train set, indiscriminately tossing pieces to the floor with loud, reverberating clacks. Losman turned back to Kat, who was now seated on his sofa, her hands folded neatly across her lap. In her navy-blue trousers, white silk blouse, and sporty wedge-heeled shoes, she looked like a woman ready to enjoy a fine brunch with her girlfriends.

"You're in a good mood," she said.

"I am," Losman said.

Kat said, "He didn't eat much for lunch and he'll be hungry soon, but he's happy to see you. He's been talking about his papa all day."

Losman smiled. Small victories like this delighted him. When Kat moved in with her Swiss boyfriend, Joachim, he was afraid the other man would become more of a father to Aksel. But Joachim, it turned out, wasn't the fatherly type; he viewed Aksel with the cool reserve a second husband might upon inheriting his wife's annoying yip-yip dog.

"Cup of tea?" he asked.

"No thanks. Joachim and I are going to Ærø for the weekend, and I have to go to the store."

Losman paused to absorb this information. Then he said, "Make Joachim go."

"You know how he is."

Losman was glad that his ex's new boyfriend was a bit old fashioned when it came to gender roles, and he took every opportunity to subtly remind her. After all, she'd broken things off with him for this guy. Ærø was a small island in Southern Denmark that he'd always wanted to visit—even going so far as to suggest it to Kat shortly after Aksel was born, when the already thin fabric of their relationship had begun to fray at an accelerated pace. He'd imagined a trip to Ærø could patch up the damage. Although it was a relatively easy trip from Copenhagen, Kat had told him she had no interest in going to Ærø with him. He'd understood this response to have the double meaning that Kat, surely, had intended. They separated for good shortly afterward.

"Do you have any plans for the weekend with Aksel?"

"We're going to the bar to pick up chicks," he said, switching to English.

"You know," Kat said, also in English. "That joke wasn't even funny the first time you said it."

"No, I guess not."

Losman jerked his head and snorted. Kat said nothing. She was accustomed to his tics. Years ago, once he was good enough at Danish to speak in complete sentences, he and Kat began using it exclusively. It was strange at first, to go from deep, intimate conversations in one language to shallow, strangulated conversations in another. Instantly he'd gone from being a college-educated quasi-intellectual to a second grader lacking the vocabulary to properly voice his thoughts. Whole levels of complexity were lost to him, leaving him periodically mute and dumb, and it had taken quite some time for him to catch up. But now he found it jarring to speak English with Kat, even in short bursts. It was impersonal and awkward, as though they were strangers meeting in a foreign country, expressing themselves in their only common language.

He'd met Kat at the Barnes & Noble in Philadelphia where he worked while attending graduate school at Temple. Kat, then a graphic design student at the Art Institute, would sit in the coffee shop with piles of design books scattered around her desk, like debris from a bombed-out building. He'd noticed her long, thick blond hair and cool aquamarine eyes long before she'd noticed him. In those days, she'd been obsessively focused on her studies, and it was only after he got to know her (she needed his help one day to find some books) that he understood why: she was in Philadelphia on a one-year fellowship from her home university in her native Denmark, and she was trying to cram as much as possible into that year.

Losman, whose constant fear of embarrassing himself in a fit of public ticcing made him shy to the point of self-effacement, attempted awkward conversation with her. As a kid he had touched things compulsively, and he was grateful that he'd mostly outgrown that habit, because if he hadn't, he would've repeatedly patted her hand or stroked her fingers, freaking her the fuck out. When he saw her in the café with her books, he would say hello in a tight, croaky voice, and occasionally let her use his store discount on coffees and muffins. One day in early April, he stood in line at the café and felt a tap on his shoulder.

When he turned to find her smiling up at him, he felt that familiar nervous flutter in his belly he always felt around her. He wanted to say the right things, but he didn't know what those right things were. "Hey there," he said, clearing his rusty throat. "Wanna coffee?"

She raised her hand and tried to hold it steady, but it was shaky. "I've had too much already. The coffee here is so strong."

"Jesus," he said, staring too long at her hand because he didn't know what else to do. He blinked a few times rapidly, his nerves besting him. "You on break?"

"Yeah."

"Will you sit with me?"

"Sure," he said, blinking.

Normally, Losman read a book during his lunch breaks, but not on this day. He sipped his coffee and listened to Kat, who seemed manic, pinballing from topic to topic. But Losman didn't mind. With her doing the talking there was less a chance that he would say something stupid, or tic. He'd been a late bloomer, not going on his first date until he was in college, and he was never very comfortable around girls. He always felt like a minor nuisance, a buzzing fly to swat away, and his motherfucking tics didn't help.

As his thirty-minute break drew to a close, Losman discovered that she hadn't been to any of the city's incredible museums. How could you spend an entire year in Philly and *not* go to the Rodin Museum or the Philadelphia Museum of Art? Even to do the dumbass *Rocky* thing all the tourists did. Seeing an opportunity, he said, "Would you like to go?" He'd steeled himself for her to say no, but to his surprise, she didn't.

They spent three hours slowly prowling the Philadelphia Museum of Art. Losman learned he had a knack for making her laugh by miming the melancholic faces in some of the paintings. Afterward, as they stood at the top of the famous stairway gazing down the Benjamin Franklin Parkway at City Hall with its massive statue of William Penn, she threaded her arm through his and he felt weightless. Without Kat there to anchor him, he would've drifted up to the clouds like a balloon. He drove her back to her dorm, and he tried to manage his tics with a periodic tilt of his left shoulder or a wiggle of his fingers. She didn't invite him up, as he'd hoped she would, but she did kiss him square on the lips and tell him she had fun. She was much bolder than Losman, a fact that was endearing to them both in those early days.

Things moved fast after that. Coffee shops, movie theatres, even Flyers' and Phillies' games. Kat was willing to go anywhere with him, as if she were making up for lost fun in this big American city. At the Mütter Museum, Losman's favorite place, Kat stared gape-mouthed and wide-eyed at the malformed fetuses floating in jars of formaldehyde. "I can't decide whether this is beautiful or horrible," she said.

"It's both."

She noticed his tics. "Why do you blink and snort so much?"

He cleared his throat and told her the truth. What choice did he have? The moment was both exhilarating and terrifying, liberating and imprisoning—locking him as it did into place as the boy with Tourette. He'd always been too humiliated by his tics to seek lasting friendships, preferring to maintain a proud, stoic distance, letting no one into his solitary bubble. But to his surprise, she kissed him. "My little weirdo," she said. "You're so cute."

That afternoon, in his cramped fifth-floor studio apartment on South 15th Street, Kat pushed him against the wall and kissed him hard. They stripped off their clothes and slurped, tugged, stroked, sucked, licked, and inspired their bodies into acrobatic knots that would've made a contortionist proud. He felt like he was on fire, burning up from within with an unquenchable desire nothing could slake. When Losman finished his graduate program at the end of that year, she invited him to follow her to Denmark, and he didn't hesitate to say *hell yes*. By that point, he would've followed her anywhere, this woman who knew him and accepted him for who he was.

But that was so many years ago now, back when he still expected to find thrills sprinkled like Golden Tickets throughout his day. Once they were coupled and living together, all the cracks began to show. Kat was ambitious in ways that Losman was not, and she worked her way up at *Kvinde* from graphic designer to Art Director within just a few years. She was outgoing and charming. She liked hanging out with friends or going to clubs and dancing until the wee small hours, while Losman's idea of a good time was a cozy evening at home watching a movie. In hindsight, it was a wonder they lasted as long as they did.

"Far! Far!" Aksel screeched. He held up the fat little Sir Topham Hatt figurine, which they'd searched in vain for the last time Aksel was here.

"That's great, buddy. Where'd you find it?"

"I kassen!"

"It was in the box the entire time? I can't believe it!"

"I'm so glad you're willing to play Thomas with him," Kat said once Aksel was absorbed in his toys again. "He talks about it nonstop. He's just like you that way, obsessive."

Losman turned away, stung at this offhand remark, even if it was true. Along with Tourette he'd been diagnosed with Obsessive

Compulsive Disorder. As a kid, he'd crossed his fingers every night from 8:32-8:37 while lying in bed because he feared that if he didn't his parents would die, and he didn't tell anyone he did this, because that would kill them too. These days, his OCD mostly meant fanatically clearing his email inbox, writing and completing endless to-do lists, and maintaining a rigid daily schedule. Failure to do these things would cause him to become physically ill.

He knew how much Kat loathed Thomas the Train—especially the way, she claimed, the cartoon trained kids to consider the value of work. That unless you were *productive* you were a drain on society. Sir Topham Hatt represented the capitalist class, according to Kat's party pooper theory, and the trains were the proletariat worker bees; it was such Anglo-American horseshit, she liked to say. But he didn't want to talk about Thomas the Train. He said, "I'm working on that, Kat. I'm going to a therapist."

For some reason he didn't care to probe, he felt a pathetic need to prove to Kat that he was doing okay.

"That's great," Kat said. "I'm happy for you." She got to her feet and picked up Petersen's book, then began to riffle through its pages. She was a tall woman with a big-shouldered density, the sheer muscular heft of a triathlete, and the frank, intimidating self-assurance of someone who knew exactly what she wanted in life and how to acquire it. No doubt this was the result of growing up in an ambitious family. Her parents owned an enormous pig farm in North Zealand and had raised their three children to understand the proper value of work (the irony of which was lost on her whenever she railed against Thomas the Train). Kat was the youngest, the only girl. None of the siblings wanted to take over the family business. One of her brothers, Per, made scads of money selling commercial real estate, while the other, Jørgen, worked in IT for the government. As far as Losman was concerned, both were assholes. When Kat imported Losman from Philadelphia, her family regarded him as a distinctly American curiosity, like a jackalope or a Big Gulp. They tolerated him at family outings, but Losman was certain that when Kat finally dumped him, they were relieved.

Losman stared at the thick blond hair piled atop Kat's head. Even now it pained him to think that she no longer loved him or wanted to be with him, that he was forever embedded in the ambered status of ex-boyfriend. Unable to contain this feeling within him, he turned away. She said, "I read about this book in *Information*. What do you think of it?"

"It's terrible."

Kat looked at Losman, her eyebrows raised. "The reviewer liked it."

"The reviewer's a dipshit. It's the worst book I've ever translated," he said. He squeezed his hand into a fist, pumped it twice. "Read it for yourself. You'll see. You can have it when I'm done."

"I'll take your word for it," she said, carefully returning it to the holder. "You're not much of a salesman."

"I'm not a salesman, I'm a translator."

"Have you written any of your own stories lately?"

"No," he said. "What's the point?"

"Why does there need to be a point? You're good at it."

"No, I'm not."

"If this book is as bad as you say it is," she said and pointed at the Petersen book, "can't you write a better one?"

Losman cleared his throat and snorted. Any discussion of his writing fiction—or his not writing fiction—aggravated him. He used to enjoy writing, but now it only reminded him what a failure he was. The best he could do was translate others' work. Like a con artist copying an original masterpiece (or in this case a bestselling sack of garbage). Sometimes, it was true, he wrote fairy tales, stories he made up when putting Aksel to bed. Those were easy, and fun, and he could whip them up in a day. But he never did anything with them, because at some point he realized that every single fairy tale he told was a kind of fractured mirror reflecting himself. *A failure, Losman. A MOTHER-*

FUCKING NAVEL-GAZING F-A-I-L-U-R-E. Fearing she would leave soon if they continued down this depressing vein, he changed topics. He wanted her to stay a while longer. It was good to have a real adult conversation for once—one that didn't require him to pay a psychologist—even if it was with a woman who'd abandoned him for someone else. "Remember that old guy who used to live in this building? Kramer?"

Kat sat down again, smoothing her trousers as she did so. "The alcoholic?"

"That's the one. He died yesterday in his apartment. Possible suicide."

"That's sad. Who found him?"

"I did."

She leaned forward in concern. "*You?* Are you okay?"

"Yeah, I'm fine. Besides, I wasn't alone. Caroline Jensen from 2V was with me."

Kat rolled her eyes. "The kooky goth girl who draws pictures?"

"That seems like a mean description of her."

"You're right—sorry. It's just that she keeps emailing me her cartoons asking if we'd publish them in *Kvinde.*"

"She does?" Losman said. This was news to him. "How do you even know her?"

"I don't. But every time I bring Aksel here, she talks to me."

"How did I not know this?"

"What does it matter? How well do you know her anyway? Are you dating her, Losman?"

He laughed and shook his head. The truth was, he didn't really know Caroline at all. They'd found a dead guy together.

"She's this nervous little thing," Kat said. "She jabbers on and on, hardly stopping to breathe. She tried to friend me on Facebook once."

"God," Losman said. He recalled the warm feel of Caroline's hand the day before, how she'd clutched his as if he were her only hope from drowning in some sea of utter misery. She had never tried to friend Losman on Facebook, and it nipped at him to think Caroline was nothing more than another eager ladder-climber looking to catch a break by stepping on people's heads. A Niels H. Petersen. Had she held his hand only because it might be a way for her to get closer to Kat? He was stunned. "I had no idea."

"It doesn't matter, Losman. There's no way we'll ever run those cartoons of hers. We publish fashion, beauty, and sex tips for women because our readers want to know how to have a better orgasm, not follow the sad life of a gloomy girl with an eating disorder. I don't think she's even read the magazine."

When Losman told her that he'd seen Caroline canter out of the building that morning carrying her oversized portfolio under her arm, Kat decided to go before she returned. Losman instantly regretted telling her.

"I didn't mean for you to leave."

"It's okay. I'll be late if I don't. Joachim doesn't like—" she began before breaking off mid-sentence, likely because she recognized how unlike the old Kat she sounded. The old Kat never would've let Losman dictate terms.

AFTER KAT LEFT, Losman kneeled down on the hard floor with Aksel. He'd play with his son until he couldn't—his endurance for play was not strong. Before long he would grow tired, bored, irritated, or all of the above. Aksel dumped the box of tracks into a pile and began slowly and methodically to link them together. Losman laid his arm on the stack and slid half the pile to him.

"You build your half and I'll build mine," he said. "We'll meet in the middle."

Losman was much less careful about which tracks he fit together or what kind of pattern they made. His objective was to create any wide, oblong, or circular shape on which Aksel could push his trains, and how that task was accomplished was hardly important to him. Aksel, on the other hand, would lift a section of track and carefully study its joins—what Losman's father would've called its male part—then stare at the track searching for the exact place to slide it into the female part. Aksel wasn't aware of this male/female analogy, of course, and Losman would never volunteer to explain it to him. Losman's father was an electrician—or had been anyway, before his Alzheimer's diagnosis— and not typically one to use metaphorical language. But this was one instance he did, and it had been permanently lodged in Losman's brain, because his father had frequently referred to plugs and sockets as male/female parts. Before Losman hit puberty, he didn't understand why. Once he was old enough to understand, he was embarrassed by his father's use of the terminology, which seemed silly. Worse, it seemed earnest and completely unsexual, as if his father truly didn't think of cocks and pussies engaged in sloppy intercourse. To this day, Losman found himself—much to his annoyance—thinking of dicks and vaginas whenever he jammed a plug into a wall socket.

A track began to emerge. It only took twenty or so minutes to complete, but it felt like an hour. Losman's knees ached, and he shifted his weight. He slowed down to watch his son grapple with the pieces. Whenever Aksel was deep in concentration, like now, his tongue lolled from his mouth. He and Kat had done one thing right, at least: they had drastically limited the amount of screen time Aksel got. He was allowed to watch thirty minutes of television a day, and on weekends— usually Fridays—a movie. As a result, he seemed far more focused than many of the other kids in his daycare, who flitted about like bonobos injected with heavy doses of sugar.

Aksel was a sturdy child, pale and blond like his mother, brown-eyed like Losman. Losman studied his movements with something like awe. The boy pressed his face close to the tracks, determined to lay them out in a precise manner. If a piece didn't fit, he didn't try to make it fit; he knew better than to do that. Instead, his small, nimble hands darted out to his ever-decreasing stack of tracks and found another that would. Realizing that Aksel no longer needed him—that Aksel was in fact so engrossed that he didn't even register his father's presence—Losman stood up and walked to the kitchen. He cleared his throat a few times and shook his head, before opening the fridge and grabbing himself a Carlsberg. He stood leaning against the countertop, drinking his beer, feeling immensely satisfied in the moment. It had been a good day—a good week—and now he had a full weekend to spend with his son.

Aksel affixed the final piece in his track, and now he stood up to admire the work: a lopsided figure eight with elongated turns and two bridges that arched over the tracks.

"Far!" he shouted. "Se!"

"That's awesome, Aksel. Great job!"

Aksel's face brightened into a broad, beaming smile, bringing dimples to his chubby cheeks. He was undeniably happy, and Losman went to him and scooped him up in his arms. He held him tight—this solid, warm little bundle who weighed no more than a bag of groceries—and kissed his forehead. He ruffled Aksel's long, floppy hair. Aksel wrapped his arms around Losman's neck and squeezed, giggling, his tiny breaths warming Losman's skin. Losman closed his eyes, inhaling the boy's sweet scent—a blend of baby powder, milk, and oranges—then tickled the boy's ribs until he squealed with delight. In this moment, hearing his son's laughter, Losman felt content. He was the father of a wonderful, healthy child and there was nothing in the world more delightful than to see him happy. A gift, it was, something precious that moved him to love his son all the more deeply. All the pain he felt, all the loss he'd suffered when Kat left him, when he imagined her in intimate embrace with Joachim, could not shake this incredible feeling he had whenever he held Aksel in his arms. He was filled with love, an abundant joy. Before Aksel came along, he'd had no comprehension of what it meant to feel such love. Now that he was awake to it, he didn't want to ever let it go.

But eventually, inevitably, Aksel squirmed from Losman's grasp and began to collect his trains. He'd built his track, now he wanted to play with it. Losman returned to the kitchen and set a pot to boil on the stove. He pulled a hunk of cheddar and a carton of milk from the fridge along with a bag of edamame beans from the freezer and got to work shredding the cheese on the countertop. Losman was a lousy cook, but Aksel liked macaroni and cheese and Losman could manage that. Kat, who was a terrific cook, never made macaroni and cheese for Aksel, so it was always a treat when he was with Losman. Which made father and son both happy. From the kitchen, Losman watched Aksel as he prepared their meal. Four years ago, when he and Kat argued—about money, about their jobs, about the petty grievances they'd gathered, like sharp stones, against each other—Losman never would've imagined he'd one day be the father of Kat's son. They certainly hadn't intended to have a baby, but they both knew it was foolish not to use protection. Even if they weren't together anymore, neither could imagine a life without Aksel. How empty it would be.

Losman stood at the counter, drinking his beer and admiring his son's play. Aksel was on his hands and knees, concentrating on the business of pushing a line of magnetically conjoined cars, with Thomas in the lead, around the track. He was monomaniacal about his play, a junior Ahab, making whirring engine noises, his lips vibrating. On occasion, Losman observed, Aksel's left cheek twitched, a hard wink, and Losman wondered what the boy was thinking about as he played with his trains. As he did *any*thing, for that matter. And what would he remember of this period in his life? Of this day? Anything at all? Losman certainly didn't remember being three years old. A child's mind was a mystery, far more so than an adult's. It was a lump of clay waiting to be stamped with impressions, while an adult's mind was already a riot of impressions, the clay twisted and knotty and hard. An adult could learn new things, sure, but the basic structure was locked in place; from birth onward patterns emerged and solidified, and these fit neatly, layer upon layer, on what was learned early in adolescence. And at some point, even that structure would begin to retreat. Like Losman's father, whose memory fought a losing battle with a hungry, gobbling monster.

The last time Losman had visited his parents in Manayunk, he'd brought his latest translation, an obscure gem of a book that he'd originally discovered while browsing a shop in a seaside resort town in western Denmark. Somehow, he'd managed to find a small independent press to publish his translation in the United States. He'd earned no money translating the stories—other than the meager grants the Danish Arts Foundation awarded him—but he didn't care so much about that. He was immensely proud of the work.

His father sat in his customary wingback chair watching a Phillies game on television, his eyes alert to the movement of the players on the screen, as if he were the old Dad who loved baseball, who could still follow the action with a whole and perfect mind. Losman sat beside him on the couch, turning from his father to the screen to his father.

"Hey, Dad," he'd said. He set the book on his father's lap. "I brought this for you."

His father glanced down uncertainly at the slender volume. "What is it?"

"It's my latest translation."

His father looked at him. Two years had passed since Losman had last flown home—he didn't have enough money to do it every year—and in that span of time his father had aged considerably. He was thin and pale and sickly, his voice soft and weak. Though he was only seventy, he looked and sounded ninety, and it made Losman sad to know that the one time he'd been able to bring Aksel home to his parents, when the boy was four months old, his father had been unable to process that this was his grandson, his first and only. Aksel would never meet the beautiful man Losman had once known. "You did this?" his father said.

Losman nodded.

"What is it?"

"It's a collection of stories. See," Losman said, opening the book to the first story, which was also Losman's favorite. His father's hands shook as though from palsy.

"Did you write this?"

"I translated it, Dad."

"You did?" Losman's father—whose name was Gary—stared openmouthed at the page. "What is it?"

"It's a book, Dad. I translated it and now I'm giving it to you."

"Thank you." Gary closed the book and stared at the cover, which depicted an overturned silver milk truck spilling its contents onto a bare country road. He seemed both mesmerized and confused by the gift.

Losman sat in silence with his father for the rest of the inning. Gary stared at the screen while absentmindedly fingering the pages of the book in his lap, but it was clear he wasn't really here, there, or anywhere Losman recognized; the light in his eyes had gone out. When the commercials came on, Losman returned to the kitchen where his mother was busy chopping vegetables for that evening's dinner. He hugged her, and she buried her face in his shoulder. Although it was difficult for him to witness the slow corrosion of his father's faculties, he was only in town for two weeks. He couldn't imagine what it must be like for his mother, who had been married to this man for more than forty years, who saw him getting worse day by day.

"He's happy to see you," his mother, Denise, said. She wiped her eyes, composing herself. Where his father seemed to be decaying from within, his mother appeared to be blooming into health. She was gray-haired and thin, but her skin was tanned a healthy shade of pink from all the hours she spent working in her garden. Losman, an only child, had always had a tight connection to his parents, who had doted on him from the start. When he still lived at home it was common for him to spend a Friday or Saturday evening, even in high school when his classmates were partying, playing Monopoly or Backgammon with them. Losman had never been outgoing.

"How can you tell?" he asked his mother.

"He doesn't watch baseball anymore," she said. She dumped a bag of radishes into a colander and rinsed them in the sink. A bird alighted on a feeder on the deck of their row house. "It's only because you're here. You two used to love it, remember?"

Losman remembered. How could he forget? His father took him to many games at old Veterans Stadium, going all the way back to Mike Schmidt, who was Losman's favorite player. For his father, Losman suspected, the baseball games were partly an excuse to drink beer from tall stadium cups on a sunny Saturday or Sunday afternoon, free from his wife's nagging commentary about afternoon drinking. Losman would hold his father's hand as they ascended the walkway up to their seats on the third level of the stadium, his body charged with the electricity of his anticipation. He always wore his Phillies cap and jersey, always brought his glove (though he never caught a foul ball), and always gasped when they exited the ramp into the great bowl of the field and beheld the bright green carpet of Astroturf, the crisp white chalk lines extending from home plate all the way to the foul poles in left and right. To Losman, this moment was magical.

"Do you think *he* remembers, Mom?"

"Maybe subconsciously? I certainly didn't turn the game on."

Losman considered the possibility that his father's subconscious had driven him to find the game, now that his son was home. Watching baseball was something they did together, every summer, without fail.

"Do you really think that's possible?"

"Sure. Why not?" his mother said. "There's a whole life buried in his head. I can't reach it, and most of the time he can't either."

"What *does* he remember?"

She began to hack up a large cucumber into thin slices, her knife striking the wooden cutting board in rhythmic clops. "Mostly his childhood," she said. "He talks about your grandparents and your aunts and uncles quite a bit. Stuff they did together." She gave him a sad smile. "I never realized your Uncle Jeff was such a troublemaker."

Losman cleared his throat. "I want to hear some of these stories."

"Don't stand here talking to me then. Go to him. He needs you now, and I think you need him too."

Losman turned to see his father holding his book, staring at it, mouth open as if completely absorbed in the story he was reading. Seeing this version of his father, Losman was filled with sadness, and his eyes misted up. He had never said *I love you* to him, or even *thank you for being such a great dad to me*. Was it too late to say these things? If he said them now, would his father understand the words? He gently removed the book from his hands and turned it right-side up. "There you go," he said, and planted a kiss on his father's bald, liver-spotted head.

THAT NIGHT AFTER DINNER, Losman and Aksel watched *Cars*. It was one of Aksel's favorite movies. Aksel snuggled against Losman, his eyes wide with wonder at the images on the screen.

After the movie, he got Aksel in his jammies and they settled into the bed. Although Aksel didn't speak much English, he understood more than he let on. He loved Dr. Seuss, particularly "The Sneetches." Losman arranged the pillow so that he could sit leaning against the wall. Aksel snuggled up against him, clutching Solly, the little plush toy he slept with every time he visited, the same one Losman had slept with as a kid. His mother had stitched it together with blue fabric on her old Singer sewing machine—this weird, lopsided doll no larger than Aksel's forearm. It had no hands or feet, just these square limbs and head and big, bulging eyes and a wide mouth in the shape of an O. Losman kissed Aksel's forehead.

He read the story. The sentences had a bouncy rhythm, a jaunty singsong flow that Losman liked to perform, and Aksel sat enraptured by the tale and the colorful drawings of the sad yellow Plain-Belly Sneetches.

"Sneetch on the beach!" Aksel said, his tone dipping one octave into a Danish-inflected English.

Losman smiled and went on. Along came the trickster figure, Sylvester McMonkey McBean, who was about to turn the Sneetches' world inside out. And when McBean spoke, Losman threw his voice, making him sound like a smarmy southern salesman. Aksel loved that. Once the Plain-Belly Sneetches got their stars, the story really got going, because the Star-bellies didn't like that at all. Old Sylvester McMonkey McBean fleeced the poor Sneetches of all their money.

"De er ikke særlig kloge, far!" Aksel said and cleared his throat.

"Nope, they're not very bright."

Again, Aksel cleared his throat.

"Are you all right, Aksel?"

"Ja," he said, and once again cleared his throat.

"Why are you clearing your throat so much?"

"Det ved jeg ikke."

"You don't know?"

Aksel shook his head, and Losman frowned. This throat clearing made him uneasy. It was one of the first things he'd done as a boy, before he was diagnosed with Tourette. He recalled his son's facial tics earlier that day.

"Do you feel an urge to twitch or clear your throat?"

"Hvad er det?"

"What's an urge, you mean? It's when you feel compelled—" he began, then stopped, knowing that Aksel wouldn't understand the meaning of the word *compelled*. He reversed course and took another route. "It's when you feel like you have to do something or else you don't feel well. Is that how you feel?"

"Nej."

Losman rolled on his side and looked directly into Aksel's eyes. "Are you sure?"

Aksel squinted at Losman, confused. He didn't respond but squeezed Solly tighter to his chest as if it were a shield.

"It's okay," Losman said. He kissed Aksel's forehead. "I love you, buddy."

"Kan du ikke læse historien færdig, Far?"

Losman laughed. "Yeah, I'll finish the story."

He finished "The Sneetches" and moved on to the other stories in the book. As he read, Aksel cleared his throat repeatedly, in the gruff, hacking way of a lifelong smoker, before gradually drowsing off. After Aksel had fallen asleep, the silence felt like a gift. Losman lay there in the dark beside him, holding his boy in a protective embrace. Even if scientists didn't know what exactly caused Tourette, Losman had read enough to know that current research pointed toward a genetic correlation. Which meant there was a possibility that he'd passed the gene on to his son. When Losman was a boy, his throat clearing and head shaking had driven his mother crazy. In no way did Losman want his son to go through what he'd gone through as a kid. The teasing, the humiliation.

He didn't want Aksel to face a life like this. What would happen to him if he went to school all herky-jerky like his father? Losman's mind spiraled out of control as he imagined Aksel in school, friendless, alone, miserable, committing suicide at age fourteen. No child should have to face this, he thought, sick with worry for future Aksel. He fell asleep holding his son close, never wanting to let go.

4

When Losman arrived at the Shawarma Factory on Monday, he saw a petite, dark-skinned woman in a black skirt, ivory blouse, and trendy purple eyeglasses. She was seated next to a pale, middle-aged man with stylishly unshaven, reddish-blond cheeks and a pot belly underneath a plain white T-shirt and blue blazer. Apart from these two, the restaurant had only a smattering of diners. The air was thick with the smell of sizzling meat and a vaporous cloud of unidentifiable spices. In the kitchen behind the bar, a man in a greasy white smock and baker's cap stood next to a huge hunk of lamb.

The woman offered her hand. "I am Pelin Akyürek."

Her hand was small, but her grip was firm, and she wore glittery rings on every single finger. "Is that a Turkish name?" Losman asked.

"Very good," she said. "And with your accent, you must be from North America. Canada or America? I cannot distinguish."

"Can I pick?"

"Ah, you must be American then. You shouldn't be embarrassed, Losman. America has much to offer the world." She regarded him with curiosity, like a specimen in a Petri dish. "You speak excellent Danish for an American."

Losman smirked, but he said nothing. By now he was used to this kind of dopey condescension. It seemed to him that many Danes viewed Americans through the lens of what they saw on TV or Hollywood films, and they always seemed shocked to discover they weren't hollow or vapid. It's why they often responded to him in English, even when he clearly spoke Danish.

Now it was the man's turn to stand and give Losman his hand. "My name is Jens Møller-Larsen, Director of the Center for Research on Addictive Personalities, or C.R.A.P. Yes, yes, I know it's a funny acronym in English." He grinned good-naturedly, as if letting Losman in on a joke, before gesturing to one of the bright orange plastic chairs. "Do sit, Losman." He stuffed his middle and index fingers into the breast pocket of his blazer, and they emerged with his business card pinched between them. He set the card on the table.

They ordered dönor kebabs. Losman watched the man in the white smock withdraw what appeared to be a small handsaw from underneath the countertop and carve thin slices from the lamb. He was a large, broad-shouldered man with dark skin and eyes and a bushy mustache. He ran the sharp blade through the meat with a heart surgeon's calm precision, and the machine ground like a blender.

"Why are we meeting here?" Losman asked, glancing around the restaurant as if searching for a clue.

Pelin said, "My brother owns this place."

"Is *that* your brother?" Losman pointed at the hulking man carving the lamb. It didn't seem possible the two could be related.

"Oh, no," Pelin laughed. "My brother isn't here today. But I like to support him."

Losman nodded. This made sense.

After that they made awkward small talk, which gradually morphed into what Losman realized was a kind of interview. Pelin and Jens were sussing him out, probing him with questions about his background, his mental state, his medical history. What trauma did you face in childhood? What trauma did your parents face? Did you grow up in a community devastated by environmental catastrophe? It felt like a doctor's appointment, an extension of the survey he'd submitted last week. But it was clear from their response to his answers that he'd aced whatever test this was, and Losman felt strangely elated. That old familiar thrill of being the good student.

Once the food arrived, Pelin said, "So why did you write to us, Losman? Why are you are interested in memory therapy?"

Losman swallowed a bite of lumpy, dry food, and told the abridged version of his life story.

"Very interesting," Pelin said. "And you think memory therapy can help?"

He shrugged. "Maybe? I've tried a bunch of things to control my tics. I don't suppose it would hurt to try this too. But to be honest, all I know about memory therapy is what I found on your notice, so can you tell me more about it?"

"Of course," Pelin said. She patted her lips with a napkin. "Are you familiar with FuturePerfect Laboratories?"

Losman shook his head.

"Okay. Let's start there. FuturePerfect was founded by Dr. Inga Stolz-Jacobsen. Do you know Dr. Stolz-Jacobsen?"

"I'm sorry, no."

"That's okay, Losman. She was a leading medical doctor at the National Hospital. Her daughter was a heroin addict. Despite Inga's best efforts to intervene and save her daughter, she watched her slowly succumb to her addiction. After her death, Inga founded FuturePerfect Laboratories. The goal, then as now, is to discover innovative solutions that substantially address addiction."

Losman sipped his beer and listened.

"Inga started with two basic questions: What if scientists could identify the gene or genes that cause addiction? And, if so, could they find a cure?"

Losman raised his hand like a student in a classroom. "This is probably a stupid question, but do genes cause addiction?"

"Not a stupid question at all, Losman. If we compared your DNA and mine, we'd find that 99.9% of our genetic material is the same.

But that 0.1% is rich with variation. A great deal of research indicates how a person's genetic makeup determines her capacity for addiction. To answer your question then, yes. Our goal, as scientists, is to find the addiction genes."

Jens set his fork down gently on his plate. He said, "In the case of Tourette Syndrome, scientists are studying a very promising gene called SLITRK1, which *may* cause Tourette to manifest. But genes are only one factor, Losman, and they're not our primary focus. Environmental factors also play a significant role in how our genes *act*. Have you read Gabor Maté, the Canadian physician who specializes in the study of addiction?"

"No," Losman said, distracted by something Jens had said. "What did you call that gene again, the one you just mentioned?"

"SLITRK1."

Losman stared at Jens, confounded. He'd spoken fast, and what he'd said didn't sound like any language Losman recognized—it was more like the mumbled nonsense someone makes while dreaming. "How do you spell that?"

Jens spelled it out for him, and Losman scrawled it on his damp napkin.

"I've never heard of that," Losman said, staring at the strange combination of letters. Silently he mouthed them, splitting the constituent parts. *Slit rick one.* "Is that really a thing?"

"Well, it's still very preliminary. More research needs to be done."

"Could this gene be edited to make me tic free?" Losman asked with a degree of excitement he hadn't realized he possessed until the words tumbled breathlessly from his mouth. "Is it legal to do that here in Denmark?"

"Gene therapy is legal here, in theory," Pelin chimed in. She leaned forward and tapped the table lightly with her index finger, like she was sending a warning in Morse code. "But we've not submitted the necessary paperwork to the proper authorities that oversee such research. So while it's *technically* legal, in actuality it is not—at least for us."

"Why not?" Losman asked.

"We're in the data collection phase, Losman. Your involvement in memory therapy would be part of that process, but as Jens pointed out, more research needs to be done on SLITRK1 to even determine if it's causing Tourette. At this time, we don't do that research at FuturePerfect."

Losman sipped his beer and imagined what it would be like to have his genome edited, as though his physical body was simply a manuscript to be perfected under the capable hands of a master stylist. How would someone edit his genome anyway? Would they cut him up with a scalpel, slice open a bone, and remove some marrow? Or would they use lasers to snip microscopic strands from the double helix of his DNA?

"Let's get back to Gabor Maté," Jens said. "He writes about how our modern society and its stressors foster our addictions. Just look around you in this restaurant," he said, gesturing godlike with his hand. "Everyone is staring at their phones. They are communicating with invisible people hundreds, even thousands of miles away. Through our modern technology we grow closer to people we don't know than to our own loved ones. We continue to stare at our phones because we are addicted to the dopamine spike we get when someone likes our posts or retweets our tweets. Silly, isn't it?"

Losman wasn't sure what to make of Jens. His cheeks were the ruddy hue of an alcoholic's and pocked with a crusty ridge of unhealthy-looking splotches, like adult acne. But sure enough, when he glanced to his left, he saw a thirty-something blond couple seated at the neighboring table staring at their glowing phones, scrolling through images with their thumbs and ignoring each other. And beyond them, three veiled teenage girls gawping at their screens.

"Why do they do this?" Jens went on. "Because they're addicts. And addiction is an illness. Big pharma develops drugs to treat people's illnesses, their symptoms if you will, without addressing the problems at the root. The *why* at the core. They earn a hefty profit at the expense of the very people they claim to heal."

"That's where we come in," Pelin said. "In our work with BhMe4, we aim to address the underlying problems at the heart of the issue. The why, Losman. Our project is to go back to the very beginning, into the rich dark soil of infancy and toddlerhood, to search for the root causes of addiction. After that we advance into later memories, a subject's adolescence or adulthood. Once we find the root, or *roots*, plural, we can consider solutions."

"What is BhMe4?"

"Babyhood Memory Extractor. It's the pill I have developed that unlocks what's stored within your cerebral cortex."

Babyhood. Was that even a word? Losman wondered. He cleared his throat. "A pill can do that?" he said. "How does it work?"

"By revealing to you the early or repressed memories you no longer have access to. It's like the Pensieve in *Harry Potter*. Are you familiar with the Pensieve?"

"No," Losman said. He picked up his fork and poked at his half-eaten döner kebab. "I haven't read *Harry Potter*. Or watched the movies."

"Oh, you should read the books, Losman! When I was a child I was absolutely enchanted by them. One of my fondest memories is dressing up as Hermione Granger and waiting in line at the bookstore with my friends every time a new book was published. The Pensieve inspired my work with BhMe4."

"So what *is* the Pensieve?"

"The Pensieve helps you see your old, forgotten memories." Pelin held his gaze with her dark eyes until Losman, uncomfortable, turned away. "You take BhMe4 to explore your innermost self. Like ayahuasca, the ceremonial brew consumed by the indigenous peoples of the Amazon basin. Are you familiar with ayahuasca?"

"I know of it."

"Well, I modeled BhMe4 on that plant. But I removed the DMT to create a synthetic version," she said. "It's much safer in pill form."

"I've heard people sometimes lose their minds taking ayahuasca," Losman said.

"This happens sometimes, yes, but there are multiple factors at play. Did they drink too much of the brew? Did they have a responsible guide leading them through the ceremony? Were they surrounded by a nurturing community? We eliminate these danger factors by maintaining a strictly controlled laboratory environment where we can monitor brain activity and react, if necessary. We call our process memory therapy for a reason. Our goal is to guide you through your memories."

Losman drained his beer and flagged down the waiter, ordering another. "Okay. But I'm not an addict. What can memory therapy do for me?"

"You have Tourette," Pelin said, "and that's a very interesting condition we're now studying too. No one really knows why people suffer from Tourette, why some develop tics like you. Sometimes people are even misdiagnosed."

Losman jerked his head, blinked, and snorted. A trifecta of tics. "My mother took me to a specialist when I was in middle school," he said. "Trust me, I've lived with this shit long enough to know he didn't misdiagnose me."

"I'm not saying he did," Pelin said. "Not at all. What I'm saying is that, with BhMe4, we may be able to explore the why behind your Tourette. There *is* a why, Losman. You present us with a unique opportunity to do some important research."

"You see," Jens said, "what's revolutionary about BhMe4 is that, if we are correct—and we believe we are—we could put it to use on numerous conditions beyond addiction. ADD, ADHD, auto-immune diseases, Tourette, Obsessive-Compulsive Disorder, even depression. Do you realize there are no tests administered to determine depression?

You can take a blood test to tell you if you have cancer or syphilis, but there's no physical test to determine if you have depression. In the medical field today, everything is data driven *except* mental illness. With BhMe4 we aim to produce verifiable data to change that. With BhMe4 we go back in time, so to speak, and find clues as to what caused these conditions to emerge."

Jens leaned forward excitedly, licked his lips, and continued.

"Imagine this scenario, Losman: You are subject X. Throughout your life you've suffered from debilitating depression, you've failed at relationships and your career, you hate yourself, and you find no joy in life. Now you're contemplating suicide. Using BhMe4, you locate in the deep well of your memories the very moments when your depression scooped you up in its talons. Maybe your mother was verbally abusive, or maybe your father was a malignant shadow, constantly sad because of some early trauma in *his* life. There are countless reasons to become depressed, Losman, but once you know *exactly* what triggered your depression, you can take steps to ameliorate the damage.

"I believe this scenario is plausible for you. Once we've isolated the trauma in your memories, the trigger that spurred your Tourette to manifest, we can treat the condition that developed as a result. What do you think, Losman?"

Losman cleared his throat. He lowered his hand underneath the table and squeezed it into a ball, pumping it once like a heartbeat. "You assume that Tourette is caused by trauma?" he asked.

"Yes, we do," Jens said, "*in conjunction* with a genetic mutation. We define trauma as a malignant, life-changing force. A series of events or conditions of existence that cause negative impacts—all giving rise to maladies such as yours. Take the case of an abused dog. Let's say it was beaten by its human when it was a puppy. As an adult, it will shrink from your touch if it believes you aim to beat it, even if you simply wish to pet it. It will cower in fear, and whimper. It's very easy to see trauma in a dog."

"But I'm not a dog," Losman said. "And nobody beat me. I'm an only child from a solidly middle-class family. My parents are still married to each other, still living in the same house, a nice house in a nice neighborhood, I didn't starve, I didn't suffer, and every Christmas I had a pile of presents with my name on them under the tree. I don't think trauma applies to me."

Jens held up his hand like a traffic cop. "Trauma can be a slow-drip process, Losman. Think of it as dark matter. Just because you can't see it doesn't mean it's not there. You may not *think* you've suffered trauma, but that doesn't mean you didn't. What we offer you is the chance to locate its source in you and functionally alter your ability to cope with it."

"You say that," Losman said. He finished his beer and thought of Marlene Tanner, her probing questions about his past and the clumsy way he answered them. "But how is memory therapy any different from psychotherapy?"

"There's a world of difference, Losman. BhMe4 allows a subject to witness their *actual* memories. It's like watching a film you're simultaneously acting in. Without the guiding hand of BhMe4, our memories are shapeless and blurry. They are untrustworthy. When we try to recall them on our own during psychotherapy, we're just tunneling in the dark as blindly as moles. We make connections where no connections actually exist."

"Losman," Pelin interrupted. She gently covered his hands in hers, causing an electric buzz to tingle through his body. "If you participate in our study, you will be transformed, trust me. Memory therapy is a powerful experience."

Losman stared at Pelin's hand, the rings on her slender fingers cool and heavy against his knuckles. Was it kosher for her to touch him? he wondered. Was she manipulating his emotions? He pulled his hands away. "Would I be the first subject?" he asked.

"No," Jens said, and nodded at Pelin. "We've both gone through the process, and others have participated in our trials, too. We started years ago using simple memory experiments with mice. But mice don't talk, of course, so they can't share their memories with us. We need humans for this work. It's a journey of self-discovery, Losman. Your fellow American Michael Pollan describes such a journey in his work on psilocybin."

"Psilocybin?"

"You probably refer to it as magic mushrooms."

Losman recalled choking down some dry magic mushrooms once in college, but he hadn't enjoyed any psychedelic adventures as he'd hoped, just stomach cramps. He watched the man in the white smock carve strips of meat off the slick, shiny hunk of lamb, which was thinner now and shaped like a cone.

"We've taken BhMe4 ourselves," Pelin said, "gone on the journey if you will, in order to serve as guides for our patients. It's like taking ayahuasca or psilocybin. How could we help you if we haven't made the journey within ourselves?"

"What if I flip out like someone on ayahuasca?"

"If you follow our instructions, you won't."

"You would be the perfect subject," Jens said. He leaned forward, glided his tongue across his lips, and then wiped his mouth with his hand. "We can guide you on your journey, but you must be willing to explore your own path."

"I don't really like taking pills," Losman said. Which was true. He didn't even like taking aspirin when he had a headache. "What if something goes wrong?"

"Nothing should go wrong," Pelin said.

Losman heard the slight hitch in Pelin's voice when she said should, the way it sounded *italicized* and hesitant—bracketed by a small measure of doubt. He asked her to elaborate.

Pelin went quiet a moment. "Ethically," she said, "I can't make any guarantees to you. How your body reacts to BhMe4 will determine the outcome. Our hypothesis is that there's a renegade gene that causes conditions such as, in your case, Tourette. It may be SLITRK1, or it may be another. Thanks to the pioneering work of Brenda Milner, Eric Kandel, and many others, excellent research has emerged within the field of neuroscience that demonstrates the significant role the hippocampus plays in memory formation and cataloguing. When new long-term memories are created, a network of neurons link together like tributaries of a river, each branch transmitting a seed of unique information to aid in formation and storage. As Jens said, with BhMe4 we believe we can isolate the environmental triggers that caused the renegade gene by homing in on specific memories. That's why Jens and I work together. I am the chemist, and he is the psychologist. This is groundbreaking research, Losman, one with the potential to radically alter your life. But it doesn't come without risks."

Losman certainly liked the idea of learning why he'd had tics most of his life. Could they really find a way to eliminate them altogether? Was that *possible*? He thought of Aksel. If what Pelin and Jens were trying to do proved true, Aksel might be spared a lifetime of ticcing, teasing, and embarrassment if they could isolate what triggered *his* Tourette. Knowing Losman's trigger, he and Kat could keep Aksel out of any damaging environmental situations. Even better, if Tourette manifested in Aksel, maybe they could edit the gene that caused it some day?

Still, he was unsettled, not quite ready to believe or commit. He didn't like taking risks, even the *idea* of taking risks: what if the pill caused his brain to malfunction and he lost his mind? "How will you know if this pill even works?" he asked.

"We will measure your synaptic responses," Jens said, "and calculate the data."

"I'm sorry, but that sounds like jargon to me."

"Perhaps," Pelin said, "but if you commit to our study, you will see." She scraped her chair back and reached underneath the table. She pulled out a brown leather briefcase and laid it down, clicked it open, and removed a sheaf of papers. "We will measure your responses when you are in a sleep state and compare the data. From this, we will extrapolate answers. If these pills are true to form, we will dive deep into your earliest memories and steer you close to the heart of them. We can, in effect, guide you like a Sherpa on a personal journey of discovery through your earliest memories." She offered the sheaf of papers to Losman.

"What are these?"

"The forms you'll need to fill out if you're interested in taking the next step on your journey. Take them home, Losman. Read them over carefully. Consider. You would clearly benefit from our work." She handed Losman her business card. "Call me when you've reached a decision."

5

OVER THE NEXT TWO DAYS, Losman went back to his routine, putting aside his meeting with Pelin and Jens and the pill that was supposed to return his infant (or babyhood) memories to him. His work, his ten pages a day, kept him focused and now he zeroed in like a hard-ass drill sergeant. *Hup, two, three, four! Hup, two, three, four!* He appreciated the pragmatic regularity of translation, the system of pulleys and levers that he manipulated like the great and powerful Wizard of Oz. The book may be awful, a choppy grind through the turbid slop of bad prose, but at least it was predictable.

But when Kat called on Wednesday to ask if he could pick up Aksel from daycare and keep him overnight since she had a tight deadline at the magazine, he welcomed the change.

It was a brisk two-mile bike ride to Aksel's daycare on Sankt Peder's Stræde, one that followed several heavily trafficked streets. When he entered the darkened womb of the daycare center, a single-story structure located inside the courtyard of a gigantic, four-block apartment complex, he found three rows of kids sprawled out on cots, napping like miniature vampires after a night of bloodsucking debauchery. The blinds were drawn, and the hall smelled like burnt toast and soiled diapers. Soft music, all tinkling cymbals and breezy pan flutes—the kind of thing Ecuadorian immigrants hawked on the *gågade*—piped through loudspeakers. Standing in the doorway, helmet clasp still fastened under his chin, he scanned the columns of sleeping heads searching for Aksel. Instead, he found the administrative director of the center, Jette Jørgensen, beckoning him from her corner desk. Losman stifled a grimace. Jette Jørgensen—always Jette Jørgensen, not Jette or Fru Jørgensen—was like one of those traffic cops blowing their whistle, making sure everyone stayed in line; her personality was a force to be reckoned with, as blunt and unyielding as a nightstick. In Losman's experience, she only ever spoke to parents to criticize them. Dutifully, moronically, he waved back, then tiptoed to her desk through the rows of sleeping children.

"Did you get my letter?" she said.

"Letter?"

"The one I sent home with Aksel last week."

"I didn't see any letter," Losman said cautiously. "It would've gone to his mother."

"Don't the two of you talk? Did she not tell you about the letter?"

Losman felt like a scolded child. "I don't know anything about a letter."

Jette Jørgensen frowned. She was a short but imposing woman, with the bulging shoulders and squat, powerful legs of a body builder. Her shiny black hair was set in a mid-sixties John Lennon-style bowl, and her dark eyes were like wet sand. "She should've told you about the letter."

Losman felt foolish talking to Jette Jørgensen with his bike helmet on. He unclasped the chin strap and tugged it off. "What did the letter say?"

"It *said* that Aksel shakes his head and clears his throat quite a bit. I'm concerned for him."

Losman pooched out his lip, thinking. Then he said, "Do the other kids tease him?"

"Not yet. But I think he should be evaluated. That's what I wrote in my letter."

"I didn't see the letter."

"Well, I'm telling you now." Jette Jørgensen shook her head in exasperation as if Losman was too daft for words. "You should talk to your ex. Sooner or later, the kids will tease him. I assume you don't want that?"

"I *do* talk to my ex," Losman said. "I can't help it if she didn't show me the letter. If you send another, can you send one to me, too?"

"We send one letter."

"You can't send one to each parent?"

"Why would we do that?"

"So that both parents know?"

"We expect our parents to communicate with one another," she said, "whether they live together or not."

Losman felt helpless, and an angry heat flushed his face. The urge to shake his head was there, it was stronger than ever, but he shoved it, held it down, pushed it into a closet and slammed the door. He turned away, searching for Aksel. "Where is he now?"

"In the playroom."

There, Losman found Aksel building an erector set all by himself, his face squinched in concentration. "Hey, buddy," he said. "We gotta go."

He packed up all of Aksel's things and hustled him outside into the sunlight, hefting him into the bike's child seat and clamping the helmet on his head. The first time he'd biked with Aksel in this seat he was afraid the boy would fall off—that the seat would come loose and deposit him on the pavement to be run over by a passing car—but he'd gotten over that fear.

"How was your day?" he asked as he began to pedal away from the daycare center. Free of Jette Jørgensen's judgmental gaze, he cleared his throat and jerked his head.

"Godt," Aksel said.

On the way home, Losman fumed. He hated Jette Jørgensen and her condescending attitude, and he felt sucker-punched by Kat for not telling him about the letter. As if she'd conspired to make him look like a complete asshole. But he was a good father, and he took a genuine interest in his son; he should have been informed. He of all fucking people. Behind him in his seat, Aksel yammered mostly to himself, occasionally interrupting his stream of words to loudly clear his throat.

AT HOME, after he'd fed Aksel cheese and crackers and installed him on the floor with Thomas the Train, Losman called Kat's cell phone.

"Why didn't you tell me about the letter?"

"Because I knew how you'd react."

"I got dressed down by Jette Jørgensen, thanks to you."

"*She's* overreacting. Don't worry about the letter, or Aksel," Kat said. Losman heard the chunky taps of the computer keyboard as she continued to work. "He's fine. It's just a phase."

"A phase?" Losman said. He kept his voice low so that Aksel couldn't hear him. "Have I been going through a phase for thirty some years?"

"This is different."

"How is it different? It's the exact same behavior."

"Losman, he's three. You weren't three when you started to tic."

"That's not the point, Kat. The point is I'm concerned. I don't want Aksel to have this."

"It's too early to tell," she said, her fingers plinking the keyboard with gusto, *tap, tap, tap*. "We just need to ignore him when he clears his throat. It'll go away, you'll see."

"It didn't for me. And you know as well as I do that he could've inherited this from me."

"It's too *early*, Losman. Please don't say anything to him. I don't want him to feel anxious."

"What about getting him evaluated?"

"Absolutely not. He'll think something is wrong with him."

"What if there *is* something wrong with him? I don't want him to go through life like this. You have no idea what it's like. Stop typing, Kat!"

Kat sighed, but the tapping ceased. "Just give it time," she said. "It'll work itself out. If it doesn't, we can take him to the doctor. Okay?"

IN BED THAT NIGHT, Aksel scooched up close to Losman, cozying into his ribs and snoring softly with Solly propped under his arm. He was a snuggler, Aksel was. Losman clutched him, feeling Aksel's breaths flutter against his T-shirt. He loved to watch the rise and fall of his son's chest, evidence that the boy's tiny, beautiful heart pumped life through his body. Aksel was, without a doubt, the greatest thing to ever happen to Losman. With his eyes closed, Aksel's small hands rested on Losman's chest, and Losman felt a painful ache there. What kind of terrible, doomed world had they brought Aksel into? This innocent child cushioned from the cruelty and catastrophe of humanity by the love of his parents and everyone around him? Who knew no trouble, strife, or pain. Whose ideal day consisted of pushing toy wooden trains around a wooden train track.

Every kid on the planet deserved a childhood like this.

But what of his tics? Losman wondered. What was that all about? Aksel's stringy blond hair had grown long and unruly. Losman gently whisked a fallen strand away from his eyes, then kissed his warm, chubby cheek. At this light touch, Aksel stirred, snoring once—a surprisingly deep piglike snort. Losman clicked off the lamp, and in the darkness, he thought once again of Jette Jørgensen. She had no way of knowing just how close to home she'd struck today. The last thing, the very last thing, that Losman wanted was his son facing a lifetime of Tourette. Deep down, he wished to believe what Kat had said was true: *It's just a phase, and it'll go away, you'll see.* But what if it wasn't a phase? What if it didn't go away? His thoughts spun wheelies in the mud, going nowhere, and he jerked his head until he felt okay. This niggling little bugbear stayed with Losman, kept him wide-eyed as his son drifted off to dreamland.

Following his meeting with Pelin and Jens, he'd googled the gene SLITRK1, but the few short scientific abstracts he'd found on the topic had been too difficult to understand. They were like reading a language he'd never studied, Arabic or Sanskrit or Old High Dutch. This much he understood: You could edit a gene in one of two methods. Germline editing involved manipulating embryos. But because it fundamentally altered the human species, making superbabies possible, germline editing was the ethically fuzzy stuff of science fiction. Somatic editing meant removing potentially harmful genes in a *living* person. Its aim was to improve the quality of life for people in the same way as chemotherapy or hip replacement surgery. Losman was thrilled to know that very smart minds were analyzing the connection between SLITRK1 and Tourette Syndrome; someday, if the correlation was confirmed, he might be able to live tic free. Aksel too—if he inherited the same gene mutation or whatever it was.

When *had* Losman started to tic? He remembered being called out publicly by Mrs. Graham, but the truth was, he must've been ticcing well before that, right? Could he have been Aksel's age? He'd once asked his mother this question; the earliest she recalled of his ticcing, she'd told him, was from around the time he'd come home from school crying after the episode in Mrs. Graham's class. Though he couldn't recall why or when, he knew answers to both questions were, if Pelin's pill worked, only a phone call away. If he could do anything to help his son, even if it meant taking pills, well, he would do it. The added bonus was that it could help him, too.

He climbed out of bed and pawed through his desk drawer until he found the sheaf of papers Pelin had given him and her business card. The papers were nothing more than a waiver, the kind of legalese he'd need to sign in order to participate. He set them aside.

She answered on the second ring. "Losman! So glad to hear from you."

"I hope you weren't in bed," he said.

"It's 8:30, Losman. How early do you think I go to bed?"

"Sorry. I'm on Daddy time. Listen," he said. He paused to give himself a chance to reconsider what he was about to say, but he wasn't going to reconsider, not now. "I want to know when I started to tic. And I want to know why. If memory therapy can help, I'll do it."

"You've made the right decision, Losman."

"When do we begin?" he asked.

"How about Friday night?"

"Friday *night*?"

"Yes. BhMe4 requires subjects to be asleep. This won't be a problem, will it?"

"I guess not."

"Good. Do you have a car?"

"No."

"Then Jens and I will pick you up at your apartment. Be ready at 10:00 p.m. sharp."

Part II

The Dark

6

ON FRIDAY, Losman was unable to concentrate on his work. Like a child's balloon, his mind drifted hither and yon on alternating currents of air. He was excited, and he was nervous. What had he gotten himself into? Even Marlene, his therapist, had expressed reservations during his session with her yesterday, telling him the story of Little Albert, the nine-month-old who'd been conditioned to fear soft toys and cuddly animals in a 1920 experiment. "Do you think Little Albert would've wanted to re-experience his babyhood memories again?" she asked him.

"Who knows?" he'd responded. "I mean, maybe he would've conquered his fear? Maybe that's how memory therapy works?"

But the truth was, he didn't actually know. How could he? He managed to translate his ten pages, but it was a slog. He shoved a change of clothes into his Philadelphia Phillies duffel and packed his toiletry kit.

As he made his way down the stairwell at the appointed hour, he met Caroline Jensen coming up with a basket full of laundry.

"Hello, Losman," she said.

"Oh, hey."

Caroline wore a rainbow tie-dye hemp hat, as brightly colored as the flag of some small and unidentifiable African nation, and her voice was chirpy, even girlish. She'd never spoken to him like this before, as though she were genuinely excited to see him, and it delighted Losman. Made him feel large and expansive. She was dressed in Bohemian rags, like the skinny girls he used to admire at Grateful Dead shows back in college: a loose knee-length skirt stitched together with squares cut from various other fabrics, flip-flops, and a tattered old blue sweater with a patch of white paint on the left forearm.

"Where are you off to?" she said, eyeing his duffel.

Losman glanced down at the bag. "I'm part of a study on memory tonight."

"Really? Like Alzheimer's?"

"Not exactly," he said. He thought of his father, who was losing his memory in great chunks. But tonight Losman—if this pill worked—was going to *retrieve* his earliest memories. "Kind of the opposite, actually."

They stood in silence for a beat. Caroline stared at her clean, neatly folded clothes, while Losman clutched the stairwell's polished wooden railing as if he might tumble into the void without it. He blinked. Before this moment stretched on embarrassingly long, he cast an anchor in a safe harbor. "Have you heard anything about Kramer?"

"No," she said. She looked at him now with her mesmerizing blue eyes, two crystals of pure Arctic ice. "You?"

He cleared his throat and turned away, unable to hold her gaze. "Do you think he had family?"

"I sure hope so."

"Me too," Losman said, too quickly. He squeezed his hand into a ball, forcing himself to look at her, and pulled his cell phone from his pocket to check the time. One minute to 10:00 pm. "I have to get going. My ride is here. If you hear anything, will you let me know? If there's a memorial or something, maybe we can go together?"

"Okay," Caroline said. She smiled. "I'd like that."

You would? Losman thought.

He bounded down the stairs in a tizzy of excitement. Jesus, what just happened? he wondered. Did he flirt with Caroline? Did she flirt with *him*?

A blue Citroën was parked at the curb when he emerged on the street, Pelin behind the wheel. Losman climbed in behind Jens.

"Welcome!" Jens said.

Losman didn't own a car, but even at night he recognized the streets from the many times he'd driven them with Kat, who did. Living in his bubble on Nordre Frihavnsgade, he often forgot how large Copenhagen was, with its old, historic rowhouses and imposing, block-long apartment complexes. They took Øster Allé to Route 19 and E47, heading toward the suburb of Ballerup. Losman was in a very good mood, thinking of Caroline's smile—and the way she'd said *I'd like that.* Definitely, she was flirting with him. But what did it mean?

Once they reached the O4, a stretch of motorway that but for its street signs in Danish reminded Losman of any suburban expressway in any American city, Pelin explained that FuturePerfect was housed in a six-story building made of reinforced steel and glass, part of a campus of start-up science and tech firms doing government-funded research, a Danish Silicon Valley. A bell donged in Losman's head, and he recalled reading laudatory articles about this campus in either *Politiken* or *Weekendavisen.* The start-ups all had smart anglicized names and competed against each another to be the hippest place to work, with ping pong tables and lounges and even, in one case, an indoor basketball court and hot tub.

They sliced through Ballerup until they came to a broad campus on the outskirts of town, where they wended along a narrow road called Innovation Lane, passing a series of clean-lined, modernist buildings in the style of van der Rohe or Le Corbusier, until they came to a brightly lit behemoth known simply as Building 8. With its straight lines and boxy, Lego-like construction, same-size blocks stacked in a neat pile, the structure looked more like a child's gigantic, glowing toy than an office building. The parking lot was empty when they pulled in, save for a white van on which was emblazoned the FP logo. The night air was cool and silent, and when Losman slammed the car door he heard its echo reverberate off the surrounding glass. He followed Pelin and Jens into a tall, arching tunnel, a kind of glass igloo. Inside Pelin swiped a key card and pneumatic doors swished open, and they entered a well-lit lobby with potted ferns and an enormous, tinkling water fountain. The lobby itself extended six floors, all the way to the top, and Losman tilted his head back to gawp at the night sky through the glass ceiling. Behind him he heard the pneumatic doors slide closed with a swoop, followed by a soft click, the locking mechanism. "Jesus," he said. "This is quite a place."

"It's our second home," Pelin said.

"Why didn't we meet here before?"

"Oh, we didn't want to bring you here until we determined you were a good fit for our project."

In silence they walked down a windowless flight of stairs to the basement, and they emerged into a long, dimly lit corridor.

Seeing all this empty space, Losman felt a nervous flutter in his belly. *What was he doing here?* "It's so quiet," he said. "Where is everybody?"

Pelin stopped. She turned to Losman as if he'd asked an incomprehensible question. "They're at home, I imagine. Why?"

"I don't know. It just feels—weird?"

She smiled. "It's my favorite time to be here."

Pelin began to walk again, her heels clicking like dropped coins. She wore the business attire of the office, black skirt and white blouse, as if showing up for work on a Friday night was a normal activity for her. Jens, Losman noted—wearing the same outfit as before: blue jeans, blue blazer, and brown patent-leather shoes—walked a couple paces behind Pelin.

Losman followed. When they came to a door at the very end of the corridor, Pelin once again swiped her key card. There was another click and this time she thrust her shoulder against the door, pushing it open.

Fluorescent tubes bloomed on overhead, revealing a simple room with a single bed in the center, a desk covered in electronic equipment with all sorts of colorful knobs and dials, and a large-screen, high-definition TV mounted on the wall.

Pelin was all business now. She said to Losman, "Please remove your clothes."

Losman's fingers trembled across the buttons of his shirt. "*All* of them?"

"You can keep your underwear on."

Losman's mouth went dry. He was too sober to undress in front of strangers, especially a woman. He jerked his head twice, quickly, before he cleared his throat. But just as he was about to tell them he'd changed his mind, that he couldn't do this, Pelin kicked off her heels and softly padded across the gray, tiled floor in her stockings. She removed a small thin laptop from her bag and gently set it on the table with all the electronic equipment. Distracted by her movements, Losman watched her split open her laptop and deftly maneuver her long-nailed fingers across the keyboard.

Jens approached Losman, getting so close that Losman could smell the minty lozenge clicking around in his mouth. "Would you like some help getting undressed?"

"No, that's okay. I'll do it myself."

Losman clumsily removed his shirt and pants. He felt Jens' eyes on him, appraising him. At last, he stood in his underwear and socks, feeling stupid. He turned to Pelin, embarrassed by his near nakedness, but she didn't seem to notice; she was laser-focused on whatever she was doing with her laptop.

Jens pulled two latex gloves and a tube of some kind of gel from a black bag at his feet. He snapped the gloves onto each hand and squirted a dollop of the transparent goo on Losman's shoulders, arms, belly, and legs. It was a foul substance, slick and slimy, and it clung to Losman's skin like baking grease. It smelled like Band-Aids.

"What's this for?" Losman said.

"It's for the pads," Jens said, rubbing Losman's bicep with vigor.

"Pads?"

"The sensors. They will provide us with data on your body's activity during sleep. This gel is so the pads won't chafe your skin."

Losman turned to Pelin as if for assistance. She was now untangling a knot of wires with small electrodes attached, carefully arranging them on the bed. They were the kind of wires used during an EEG.

Jens knelt at Losman's feet, his face uncomfortably close to Losman's crotch, his thick, strong hands cupping Losman's right thigh like it was a Christmas ham.

When Losman was lubed up, Pelin yanked back the duvet and asked him to get comfortable on the bed. Slowly, like a man stepping inside a cannon, preparing to meet an uncertain fate, he climbed into bed and lay down on his back. Pelin immediately began to place the sensor pads, oval strips of skin-colored mesh the size of a child's ball, on Losman's arms, legs, and chest. Once the first ten sensors were in place, Pelin asked him to roll over so that she could apply the same number to his back. When that task was complete, she had him stare at the ceiling so that she could affix the electrodes to his scalp.

"There," Pelin said when at last she'd finished prepping him. "Are you comfortable?"

Losman looked at all the doodads, gizmos, and wires connecting him to one of the machines in the room. What kind of data were they planning to harvest from him? he wondered. "I feel like a cyborg."

Pelin smiled. She folded the duvet over him and tucked him into bed, a motherly gesture that Losman found soothing, in spite of the sensor pads and electrodes. "You'll forget the electrodes are even here," she said.

Losman didn't believe that was true.

Jens lifted the black bag and set it on a table opposite the bed. He unzipped it once again, then rummaged around inside until he found a pill bottle. He examined the bottle by the light before handing it to Pelin. She didn't waste time inspecting the bottle, but simply popped the top and upended it so that one large yellow pill dropped into the palm of her hand. Losman raised himself on his elbows and craned his neck to get a better view.

"Would you like a glass of water with it?" she asked him.

He nodded.

Jens went into the adjacent bathroom and Losman heard the tap running. A moment later, he returned with the glass of water, which he handed to Losman.

"What can I expect?" Losman asked, buying himself time. He was in pretty deep now, and he didn't see any way out of taking that yellow pill. He jerked his head, snorted.

Pelin said, "When you fall asleep you will see amazing visions. But they will not be dreams, which are fantastical in nature, kaleidoscopes of random images. These will be memories."

"But they will not be ordinary memories," Jens added. "The easily recalled ones that lie on the surface. No, these will be deep memories of the time before memories solidified into memory.

"The primordial soup of memory, if you will. BhMe4 unites them again by re-firing the synaptic links to allow the neurons to pass through once more, thus presenting the memories to you—much like viewing a film in a dark theater."

"I get that," Losman said, "but how will it know the difference between stuff that happened last week, say, and when I was a baby?"

"Short and long-term memories are stored in different places in the brain, Losman."

"*I* know that, but how will the pill know that?"

"Imagine it as a key," Pelin said. "It will only unlock certain doors."

Losman nodded. That wasn't really an answer, but it was probably the best one he was going to get. It wasn't like he could possibly understand all the pharmaceutical mumbo jumbo involved in actually developing the pill anyway. "How will you guide me?" he asked. "Will you be there? Like some kind of narrator?"

"Not exactly. We can't go *with* you. You will be in a place with your babyself."

"My what? *Baby*self?"

"You will understand soon enough," Jens said from the corner of the room where he stood looking on.

"Yes," Pelin said. "Your babyself. You will see what he sees. We'll discuss it in the morning. This is how we'll guide you through your memories. Remember, we've taken this journey ourselves." She paused and touched Losman's hand. "Losman, you are about to begin a wonderful journey of discovery. Trust me when I say this might be one of the strangest and yet profoundest journeys you will ever undertake. But that journey is not always a straight path."

Losman wasn't sure he wanted to do this anymore. To steady his nerves, which had flared up again now that he resembled some hapless low life in a Philip K. Dick novel, he closed his eyes and counted to five. He waggled his fingers, balled his fists, cleared his throat, and jerked his head. A terrible thought struck him. He said, "Those stories about people going crazy on ayahuasca. Do you promise that won't happen to me?"

"We're giving you a very specific dosage, Losman. You'll be fine if you do *exactly* as we tell you."

"Are you sure?"

"I'm sure," Pelin said reassuringly.

Although Losman didn't know how Pelin could be so sure, he decided it was a pointless question to pursue. "What are you two going to do while I sleep?" he said. "You're not going to *watch* me, are you?"

"Will that make you uncomfortable?"

"Kind of, yeah."

"It is okay. We leave the room. You are now linked to our network, so we can observe your metrics from the control center. If you are uncomfortable, it will skew the results. We don't want you to be uncomfortable." Pelin thrust her hand toward him, on the palm of which, resting like a giant bug with a hard, yellow shell, was the pill. "Before we go, you must take this."

Losman hesitated. He turned from Pelin to Jens, searching their faces for signs, of what, exactly? Hilarity? Evil? Earnestness? After all, he didn't even know them. When he didn't immediately take the pill, Pelin pushed it closer to his face. Finally, he plucked the pill from her hand, daintily using his thumb and forefinger. He examined the thing carefully, its cylindrical shape, its smooth contour. Four letters and one digit, BhMe4, were carved into it. He looked at Jens, who nodded his head slowly, a gesture Losman understood to mean, *Go on.* "What if something goes wrong?" he said. "Will you know?"

"We will know. That's what all the sensors are for. The electroencephalogram measures your brain activity."

"And you will return?"

"Immediately. We will be nearby."

Jens said, "As soon as you swallow the pill, we will leave the room."

Losman exhaled and slid the pill into his mouth. It felt weightless on his tongue, no more substantive than a single kernel of corn—like any other pill. He guzzled his glass of water.

"Sweet memories," Pelin said. A bright smile finally emerged on her face, and for the first time Losman noticed that her teeth were a little crooked. But the smile itself was genuine, happy, and for a dark, childish instant, Losman feared it was the terrible grin of a serial killer who'd just conned another victim to his death.

PREDICTABLY, LOSMAN COULD NOT SLEEP in this strange room deep in the bowels of a peculiar glass and steel box. And all these wires and pads connected to his body aggravated him, reminded him that he'd swallowed a pill given to him by virtual strangers; that he was a *test subject*; that he'd signed a waiver indemnifying Jens and Pelin and FuturePerfect Laboratories from any wrongdoing should something in fact go wrong. So far, he'd noted nothing out of the ordinary: no dizziness, nausea, or discomfort. Maybe the pill was no more harmful than aspirin? Maybe it was a dud? Maybe Pelin was a horrible pharmaceutical scientist?

He felt a twinge of disappointment, too.

He glanced longingly at the television—or where he knew it was affixed to the wall, since he couldn't see much of anything in this pitch-black room. He wanted to turn it on, to pass the time if nothing else. The remote control was beside the bed, somewhere; finding it was a simple matter of lifting his right hand and pawing around on the nightstand. But he wasn't allowed to watch television. Strict orders. Before Pelin had left, she'd told him that he must do nothing but sleep. He couldn't even stand up and walk around the room, not even to piss. Any activity besides sleep would skew the results, she said. This was her favorite phrase.

"Not even television?"

"If you watch something disagreeable, we will see an endorphin spike."

"Or if you watch something *agree*able," Jens added.

"Yes," Pelin agreed. "If you watch any television at all, you will skew the results."

So here he was, lying motionless but for the occasional head jerk and snort at something o'clock in the morning, willing himself to sleep and failing. Wondering how he'd got himself into this spot. Without his eyeglasses, the shapes in the room were lumpy and indistinct, and he felt a slightly discomfiting sensation that he imagined was akin to what an astronaut feels floating adrift in outer space. He knew what objects were in this room only because he'd seen them with the light on. At the center of the room, like a guiding North Star, were the glowing digits of the television clock, blurred to a runny smear of neon green.

The only thing left for him to do—to Hell with Pelin's orders—was listen to the audiobook he'd downloaded to his cell phone. After Jens and Pelin had left, he'd fumbled in his duffel for his phone and earbuds and set them on the stand next to his bed in case he couldn't sleep. He didn't like listening to audiobooks at night, because the drone of the voice in his ear always put him quickly to sleep. The next morning, he would have to replay the entire chapter. But he didn't care about that now. All he wanted was to sleep; the sooner he fell asleep, the sooner this entire episode would be over. He jammed the earbuds into his ear, pulled up the app, and pushed play on John Le Carré's *Tinker, Tailor, Soldier, Spy*. Within minutes, lulled by the mellifluous, rich baritone of the British narrator, he fell into a fitful but welcome sleep.

A YOUNG VERSION OF HIS MOTHER APPEARED along the fuzzy rim of his consciousness. She had short dark hair and smooth, copper-toned skin. She was holding him, and he was scabbling at her shirt with his jerky newborn hands. The smell of milk, fragrant and rich, guided him to his destination. A powerful hunger gnawed in the pit of his gurgling stomach. His body trembled with pleasure when his lips found her nipple and latched on, leechlike. He tugged and pulled and suckled and yet no milk gushed forth. His mother began to cry. And he understood why, sensed it with the impact of an absolute truth: desperation. She was desperate, afraid she would be unable to nurse her baby, afraid she would fail as a mother. Once he understood this, something in him altered, the joy he'd felt only moments before rushed away and was replaced by an animal urge to feed. Hunger beckoned, hunger threatened, and he too began to bawl.

The scene shifted, and he was lying on his back on a mattress. There were indeterminate shapes to his right and left, dark stationary objects that scared him. Him, yes. They scared him, but not the adult him: the *baby* him. Somehow, he was conscious as a baby *and* as an adult, with his learned ability to comprehend and evaluate. As if his adultself were inside his babyself. Just as Pelin had said. The baby him was staring gape-mouthed, awestruck, pleasantly entertained by the rotating fan on the ceiling as it whirred around and around and around and around. A gash of sunlight sliced the room beyond the periphery of his vision, causing a perpetually circling shadow to cling to the blades of the fan. In the distance, he heard voices, garbled as if pouring through a filter. They were speaking softly, then louder. Louder. LOUDER. He did not understand the words. Adult him understood the words, but they were removed from context and shorn of meaning. Baby him, frightened by the angry voices, began to wail inconsolably.

And then: a square of light. White walls. A wiggly hand before his unfocused eyes. Baby him was confused. He felt he was moving, but where? How? At once adult him understood. The white walls were part of a carriage, the square of light the sky. The hand, his. It was a pleasant sensation. His eyelids sagged closed.

And jolted open to the sight of a woman pushing a tiny toy alligator in his face. Baby him screamed. Adult him screamed. Though she was much younger, he recognized his mother immediately. The long, brown hair cinched back in a ponytail. The chunky plastic eyeglasses that made her appear forever trapped in the year 1976. The moony cheeks dotted with freckles. The voice cooing: *hullo, little baby. I love you so much, little baby.* A man's perplexed and weary face appeared, his father's.

Next he found himself staring into a potty at a perfect log of brown poo the length of a cigar, evidently his own creation. It was a jarring shift, and he smelled the thickly sweet odor of his toddlerself's emptied bowels. His mother was kneeling beside him. His toddlerself was holding her hand—he could feel its warmth, its loving tenderness cupping his. She said, in a chirpy, high-pitched squeal of delight, "Very good, Daniel! You pooped in the toilet all by yourself!" And then he saw her hand lifting the potty, dumping its contents into the toilet.

"We have to flush it now, okay?" she said, pushing the handle down. The water in the toilet filled and swirled, whirlpooling the brown log around and around until it was gone.

"Bye-bye, poopy," his toddlerself said, waving.

A new scene. One by one the people emerged, staring at him momentarily—cooing and gagahing—before slipping like eels back to wherever they had come, to be quickly replaced by others. Baby him reeled in terror, screeching at the top of his lungs. But adult him was calm, adult him understood, adult him was resigned to watch the endless parade of faces emerge and disappear. They were his parents' friends. There goes younger versions of Mr. Beckwith and his wife Deedee; there goes his dad's colleague John Janowitz with his wife, Cindy. One after the other they came, saw, and moved on.

Soon he faded from the scene and reappeared somewhere else. Where? He was lying on his back, and could see his naked, chubby little legs kicking and sprawling at the air. A bright light glowed directly above, which adult him quickly recognized as a panel of fluorescent bulbs. The walls were bare and artificially white, like in American television commercials, scrubbed and neutered. A man appeared dressed in a blue hospital gown and surgical mask, and he approached baby him. He was deeply tanned, with skin smooth as amber, and perfectly coifed white hair. Pinched between his slender fingers was some kind of metal device. He leaned over baby him, out of sight. Then: searing pain, the worst Losman had ever known. Baby him howled; adult him howled. He could feel his body go rigid, a dizzying, teeth-clenching agony that dropped him from his own memory.

And he woke up.

IT WAS MORNING NOW. A thin circle of artificial light shined directly in his eyes, and he jerked his head away, squinting. Though his vision was blurry with sleep, a little groggy even, he turned to see that Jens was sitting on the side of the bed. He was holding Losman's hand in his fat, clammy fingers. Losman wrenched his hand free. "What are you *doing*?" he said.

"I was helping you through. You screamed."

Losman blinked, trying to make sense of what he'd seen and heard. To understand why this man was holding his hand. He felt sluggish, blunt headed, his thoughts lagging two or three ticks behind. He cleared his throat. "What's going on?" he said, confused.

"You had memories, yes?"

"Yeah," he said. "Well, I had something."

"Shall we discuss them?"

Losman said nothing. He'd become aware that the duvet was lifted up, tent-like, at his waist. An instant later he understood why. He had a boner, a woody to end all woodies.

Jens had also noticed. "A side effect," he said.

"Jesus."

"Would you like some water?"

"I'd like these wires off me," Losman said, and began yanking at the electrodes affixed to his scalp. "And where are my glasses?"

Jens stood. "Let me help you."

Once the wires and the mesh pads were removed, Losman shoved the duvet off and leaped out of bed, his erection squeezed painfully against the fabric of his underwear, straining to break free. He leaned forward to ease the pressure and looked down, his flag raised to full mast. He adjusted himself. "How long will this last?"

Jens handed him his glasses. "I do not know."

"You don't *know*?" Losman said. "I can't walk around like this."

"Sit down. Please. Let's talk about your memories. It will help."

"How will it help my erection!?"

A moment later, Pelin entered the room, her hair pinned up in a ponytail. She looked at Losman and her eyes immediately traveled down the length of his body to his erection. A quick glance, clinical and scientific, was all she gave it.

"Did you note the erection in the findings?" she asked Jens.

"I did," he said.

"We must continue to monitor its progress."

"Yes."

"Wait a second," Losman said, quickly covering himself with his hands, "you're talking about my dick! What about *me*?"

"Please lie down," she told Losman. "Let's not get hysterical. I'm going to the cafeteria for a coffee. Would you like one?"

A coffee actually sounded good to Losman, so he nodded. Pelin left. He rubbed his eyes, perplexed, and turned to Jens as if for answers.

"She's right," Jens said. He pulled a small silver object from his blazer pocket. At first Losman thought it was some kind of remote control, but then he realized it was one of those recording devices journalists use to interview their subjects. "It's best for you to lie down. Let's talk about what you saw last night."

Losman returned to the bed and slid under the duvet. Once he was settled in, he lifted his knees to hide his erection.

Jens waved the recorder. "Do you mind?"

Losman heard the quiver of excitement in Jens' voice, the barely concealed glee.

"I don't mind, but shouldn't we wait for Pelin?"

"Perhaps," Jens said, his voice strained, impatient. He pressed a button on the recorder and set it on Losman's bed. He picked up his pen and a clipboard, and he kept clicking and unclicking the pen.

"Must you do that?" Losman asked.

Jens pursed his lips but managed to set his pen down on his clipboard.

When Pelin returned with plastic cups clenched in each fist, filling the room with the pleasant aroma of coffee, Jens didn't even wait for her to sit on the edge of Losman's bed.

"So, tell us what you saw."

Losman cleared his throat. "I saw my mother on the day I was born." He closed his eyes and her melancholic face returned to him.

"What was that experience like?"

"Well, she was anxious. Desperate, really."

"How do you know?" Jens asked.

"It surrounded her like an aura. I could *feel* it."

Jens scribbled furiously in his notebook.

"It was incredible," Losman said. He told them about the Beckwiths and the toy alligator and the Janowitzes and the circumcision; it all just flowed out of Losman's mouth in one thrilled narrative stream. He felt like a kid at his own birthday party. "But how do I know these aren't just vivid dreams or hallucinations?"

"Dreams are incoherent, Losman. What you're describing sounds like a series of memories, which is exactly what BhMe4 was created to find."

"Are they *real* memories?"

"I certainly didn't implant anything suggestive that might lead you to have false memories," Pelin said.

"Then I guess it worked, it really did. Holy shit!" he said. "Do you know what the amazing thing was? The truly amazing thing? I had both an adultself and a babyself, just like you said, and I could see and feel in both selves *at the same time*. Talk about weird."

Pelin paced the floor, ponytail bobbing. "BhMe4 is designed this way. Babies have poor eyesight, and their synapses lack density, meaning it is impossible for them to understand and retain information. But adults have dense synapses—imagine a thick cluster of arteries—which help them store data. We need an adult to, how can I say it, *supervise* the child's memory."

Jens nodded. "What else did you see?" he said.

Losman didn't answer. He was thinking of his mother, how anxious she looked.

"Losman?" Pelin said, squeezing between him and Jens and squatting down at his side. "Hello? Losman? What else did you see?"

Pulled from his reverie, Losman looked up at her. Their faces were inches apart, so close that he could smell the coffee on her breath, and he could see finger smudges on the lenses of her eyeglasses.

"The erection!" Jens said suddenly, triumphantly snapping his fingers and gesturing at Losman's crotch, "must be the outward manifestation of your latent sexual desires for your mother. Of course!"

Losman groaned, rolling his eyes. "Don't give me that bullshit."

"The circumcision is therefore—"

But Losman held up his palm and cut him short. "I read Freud in college, Jens. He's wrong."

"You're hardly an expert in the matter," Jens said. "I have a PhD."

Losman laughed. "I hardly *need* to be an expert, Jens. I don't have an erection because of my mother. It's the pill. It's better than Viagra!" Losman peered under the duvet. When he pulled his penis down with one finger, it sprang back up like one of those weighted punching balloons he'd had when he was a kid. "Man, I haven't had a boner like this in a long time. I wonder when it will go down."

"Give it time," Pelin said.

"Time?" Losman said, smirking. "*That's* the remedy?"

"I'm sorry. We've never seen this reaction in a subject," she said.

"Let's move on," Jens said, clearly eager to probe Losman further. "How does seeing your mother make you *feel*?"

"I'm not sure how to describe it."

Jens said, "The birth moment is perhaps the greatest single experience a person can have in life—and yet we don't remember it. Why else would BhMe4 bring it out?"

"I assume that's a rhetorical question," Losman said, settling into his pillow. His erection, he realized, was beginning to soften.

"Birth is a powerful psychological event," Pelin said to Jens, all smiles.

"It's hardly a surprise that BhMe4 would pull out *that* memory first."

"Technically," Losman said, "I didn't see the birth moment." He took a pull from his cup, imagining what it would be like to become a slick, wrinkly baby squirming free from his mother's vagina. *Jesus,* he thought. *That would be a wild ride.* The coffee had little flavor, but it was hot, and it hit the spot. "How does BhMe4 work anyway?" he asked. "These memories were great and all, but I want to find out why and when I started to tic. How do I do that next time?"

Next time. He was already excited about next time.

"Partly it's dosage," Pelin said. "We gave you enough tonight to take you back all the way to the very beginning. But as we move forward in this process, we'll alter the dosage so that you'll see forgotten memories from different eras of your life. This is critical, because searching memories is a lot like finding a needle in a haystack. We don't know *when* the triggering events occurred. You'll also need to focus directly on your tics."

"So I'll be able to see Mrs. Graham again?"

"In theory, yes."

"His erection is gone," Jens said, staring openly at Losman's groin.

Pelin nodded and cast a glance at Losman's lower half. "How long did it last?"

"One hour and nine minutes. I wrote it down in the notes."

Losman spat out his coffee. "What?"

Jens said, "That's superhuman, Losman."

"It was the pill, not me."

"Maybe," Pelin said. "We'll see what happens next time. But I think the erection was *your* reaction to the pill."

"Isn't that the same thing?"

Pelin shook her head. "Every person reacts differently. Jens sweated profusely."

"Like a triathlete in the middle of a competition!" Jens said.

"I was a crier."

"Well, when can I do it again?" Losman asked. He wanted to pull out more memories from the lockbox inside his brain. "Can I do it tonight?"

"No, not tonight. We must wait one week, Losman. This is not the kind of pill you should take every day."

"Why not? Is it addictive?"

Pelin yawned. "No, it's not addictive—at least not physically. But it's a very powerful drug, and we need to administer it to you in controlled intervals. Otherwise, we can't guarantee your safety."

7

IN GRAD SCHOOL, Losman and his fiction cohort once threw a "sex scene party," the kind of shindig only a bunch of haughty creative writer types would even think of, let alone throw. People were asked to bring a book with their "favorite" worst sex scene. They'd read the passages aloud, and they'd each get a score. Like gymnastics, the ideal score was a perfect 10, only in reverse; you were rated on how terrible the passage was, so the worst passages netted the highest scores. Whoever had the most points at the end of the evening was declared the winner. Losman couldn't recall who'd won, or even which author had written the worst scene, but he'd placed second with his selection, a sample from a collection he no longer remembered but which had made sex seem as thrilling as a televised chess match. After that evening, everyone at the party solemnly declared they would rather die than write a sex scene.

Which was why Losman paused now in his work. He'd reached a scene in which the protagonist, Niels P., had trailed one of his suspects, Katrine Bredesen—a femme fatale with a mysterious past (because don't all femme fatales have a mysterious past?)—to a swank restaurant in central Copenhagen. There they sat drinking cocktails at the bar. Niels P. asked a series of probing questions ("Where were you on the night of...?" "When was the last time you...?") that before long took on a tinge of sexual innuendo. Soon, in a weird and highly implausible twist, Niels P. escorted the femme fatale to the men's room, where they proceeded to have hard, kinky sex in one of the toilet stalls as Niels P. *continued* to ask probing questions of his suspect.

Losman banged his head on his desk. What was he going to do with this trash? It was the silliest sex scene he'd *ever* read—on a scale of 1-10 it would score a 20—and yet his name would be attached to it forever. Without a doubt, once the judges for *The Literary Review*'s Bad Sex Award read this passage, they would burst into tears of laughter and shoot it up to the top of the list. He'd be a laughingstock; or, worse, readers would think it was so bad that he, the translator, must've really messed something up. The phrase "lost in translation" never failed to irk Losman, and in this instance it would be particularly galling. Though it was only his first pass through the novel, and it wasn't time to worry about syntax, grammar, awkward phrases, or mixed metaphors, there was only so much he could do with this shit. Losman hadn't replied to Niels H.'s email—his strategy was to ignore him until he went away—and got lucky when Niels H. followed up with another email, explaining that he was heading to Corsica to finish his next book but that *he absolutely wanted to see some pages when he returned.*

It was a small reprieve. But according to Losman's schedule, he still had sixteen days to finish the first draft.

This one little scene was a microcosm of everything that was wrong with this terrible book, and Losman could imagine what his UK editor—a staunch feminist with a bell hooks quote tattooed on her forearm—would say to this rot. And what about critics and readers in the English-speaking world? That particular battering ram would topple Petersen's fragile ego, a castle apparently made of papier-mâché. A whole team of sycophants at Ariadne had led him to believe in his own greatness, and in doing so had failed him. Why had they not told him that this scene was thoroughly, one hundred percent ridiculous? That Niels P. could not have sex with a suspect just because she was hot?

How was Losman going to fix it? How *could* he? For better or worse, he was stuck with it. He imagined that Petersen had concocted this scene with an overheated film version by Lars von Trier in mind. Surely, he would object to any changes.

Losman went to the kitchen and poured himself another cup of coffee. Upstairs, some kind of saw churned to life, and he thought, *oh great, just what I need.* He glanced at the clock and jerked his head a few times, puffing air over his upper lip. It was only 9:30. Below on Nordre Frihavnsgade, he searched for any distraction that could keep him occupied, away from the hideousness that awaited him once he returned to his desk. He watched an elderly man walking his golden retriever. The dog was clearly a puppy; it strained at its leash, forcing the man to stumble dangerously forward, as if blown by a strong wind. A bicyclist rode past on the opposite side of the street, heading in the wrong direction, her blond hair bobbing on her shoulders. He noted the red van parked at the curb: *Jakobsen og Sønner, Tømrer.*

His mind strayed back to BhMe4. Over the past three weeks, Pelin and Jens had picked up Losman in Pelin's little blue Citroën and driven him to FuturePerfect Labs, stuck him with pads and wires, and given him the yellow pill. Each week, more and more of Losman's babyhood life emerged. His recalled memories included his first birthday party, a beautiful day for his babyself. But as his babyself squealed through the unwrapping of his presents, adult Losman observed Uncle Glen getting drunk and flirting with a waifish, dark-haired woman that definitely wasn't Aunt Bernadette. The memory caused Losman to reevaluate his favorite uncle; now, his mother's oft-snide remarks about Glen (which he recalled even without the use of BhMe4) suddenly made sense. The man was a philanderer, a fucking asshat. Another memory, which must've been stored in his brain shortly before his first birthday party, was the moment baby Losman learned how to walk. He watched his babyself reach out and clutch a cushion on the couch. Hand over hand he moved from one end of that couch to the other, while repeatedly glancing up at his mother, delighting in the giddy clucks she made. His father stood off to the side filming, creepily silent; adult Losman recognized this scene from the home movies he had viewed years later. This had been a very happy memory. Even adult Losman cheered his babyself on.

But the memories weren't all rosy. Adult Losman saw a pattern emerge; his memories fell into one of four categories: fear, anxiety, happiness, and confusion. Not surprisingly, the memories he liked least involved fear. Like the one in which he lay alone in his bed clutching Solly. In this one he was a toddler, and no longer sleeping in a crib. His bedroom was dark but for a nightlight, and the shadows formed by that light stared at him, a forest of creepy eyes. Toddler Losman whimpered at the darkness, watching the shadows shift and glide like ghouls. The toddler's fear caused even adult Losman, who of course was traveling with him, to be afraid. Why was the toddler afraid, though? Why would a child fear darkness if he knew of nothing but light?

And there was the one in which his mother screamed at the sight of an enormous, hairy spider crawling up her pant leg. In this memory, Losman was around three years old, and adult Losman could actually *feel* his child self shrivel up in deep-bone fright once his mom leaped from her seat and frantically swatted at the spider in a state of accelerated panic. Was this the reason he hated—and kind of feared—spiders?

In this formative memory Losman had been Aksel's age. Relived moments like this were exactly what Aksel *lived* every single minute of every single day. What fears and anxieties were he and Kat inadvertently passing on to him?

Following each session, Losman woke up with an erection, though less intense than the first time, as if his body was adjusting to the pill's effects. Ever since that first session, Losman had felt a strange disconnect between his sleeping and waking selves—a growing sense of unreality. As if real life happened only when he was on the pill. That wasn't quite right, but Losman struggled to accurately explain the sense to Pelin and Jens. He'd become so fascinated by the memories he was reliving that sometimes he felt as if he were still *inside* those memories even when he was awake. That his waking life was a memory.

He dwelled on his memories so much that he'd become obsessed with them. He now kept a detailed journal. Some men watch porn, they can't help themselves, it invigorates them, but Losman had become addicted to reliving his newfound memories. Not a physical addiction but a psychological or emotional one. Which, he thought, was ironic given FuturePerfect's mission to eradicate addiction.

Although he went through the motions of his waking life, his translation work, his days with Aksel, and his meetings with Marlene, what he longed for more than anything was his Friday nights at FP when he could take the pill and ride the crest of his memory wave all the way back to his childhood. Thinking about his journeys to his past self was a pleasant diversion from his work on this putrid novel, the way he was both present and absent as the images spooled through his brain, having an out-of-body experience while simultaneously watching himself on that old television program *This is Your Life*. Following the initial grogginess after a session, his entire body absolutely thrummed with a low-grade buzz for hours. It was like being a child on the night before Christmas. He was too excited to sleep.

In two days, he would do it again. Two days seemed like an eternity. Where on Memory Lane would he go this time? During the course of four weeks, he had never, not once, had any memories involving how or when he'd developed Tourette, but he'd also been reliving *only* memories of his earliest life—up to the age of three. Pelin had promised to adjust the dosage so that he might see more years, but she also stressed patience. "We have to go slowly, Losman," she'd said. "We don't want to accidentally skip over the triggering events."

Losman was getting antsy. What he wanted, more than anything, was to revisit Mrs. Graham's classroom on the day she humiliated him.

He returned to his desk and sat down, closing his eyes, inhaling, exhaling. He cleared his throat and jerked his head until he felt stable, ready to work. When his urge was sated, he ran his palm over the nape of his neck and cleared his throat again, preparing to dive back in. But when he opened his eyes, he spotted his literal translation of the femme fatale's final remark and was thrust back into a state of unbearable misery: *Come now, big boy.*

Losman rubbed the kinks out of his neck. He lifted the book from its holder and flipped to the next page. He didn't like to scoot ahead when he translated, preferring to feel exactly what a reader might page after page, wanting that element of surprise that delighted him with fiction, but this story was so telegraphed that he already knew what would happen next: the scene would end, and in the next there'd be a dead body. And that body would belong to Katrine Bredesen, the suspect who was nothing more than a beautiful red herring the protagonist could fuck and discard, not a flesh and blood woman but a device—the last in a long chain of them in this blowhard of a novel. Later, there'd be a eureka moment when Niels P's split-personality was discovered to be the killer, so all this was just an artificial set up for the most ludicrous plot Losman had ever encountered. And he wondered, not for the first time, if Niels H. Petersen was a psychopath.

Just as he was about to return to his translation, the saw roared to life again. It was a grating sound, a heavy mechanical whirring. He waited for it to finish, took a deep breath, and settled his fingers on the keyboard.

Then came the hard *thwack* of a sledgehammer.

And the saw. And the sledgehammer again.

Jesus Christ, Losman thought. When he worked, he needed absolute quiet, and if this continued his day would be shot. He pulled on his pants and stomped up the two flights of stairs to Kramer's old place. The saw was running again; Losman could hear its sharp metallic teeth grinding wood into chips. He rapped on the door and waited, and when it didn't open, he knocked again. This time he banged with the heel of his hand and the saw died.

A moment later the door was flung open, and a young man stood before him. "Yeah?" he said. He was a freckled kid of around twenty, tall and gangly, with short ginger hair, the narrow, angular face of a scarecrow, and a prominent Adam's apple that looked sharp enough to sever wire. He wore the customary blue overalls of Danish workmen everywhere, the kind with a million pockets.

"I'm trying to work," Losman said. He cleared his throat but didn't dare jerk his head, which was what he really needed to do. "Do you have to make so much noise? It's only 9:30."

The young man shrugged. "We're working too," he said.

"Is there any chance you can work quietly?"

"Who is it?" called out a gruff voice within the apartment.

The young man turned and shouted, "It's one of the neighbors!"

Losman heard heavy footfalls, and the door opened wide. An older, balder version of the young man appeared. His face was creased with deep lines under his eyes and on his cheeks, and he had an imposing belly that strained at the buttons of his blue overalls, but it was surely Jakobsen himself.

"I'm trying to work," Losman repeated. He kept his tone measured and polite. "Is there any way you guys can be quieter?"

"*Quieter?*" Jakobsen said, and chuckled. He gestured at the pigsty that was Kramer's apartment. They'd removed the cabinets and sink and countertop from the kitchen, and these were now scattered across the living room, apparently awaiting demolition. A 2x4 balanced on a pair of sawhorses. "This isn't exactly a quiet job. Look at this place."

Losman heard the click-clack of footsteps ascending the stairwell behind him, but it wasn't until he noticed the father and son's faces—mouths open, eyes wide—that he turned to see Caroline dressed like a man. He did a double take and realized she wore a period costume from the 1920s: gray trousers, black blazer, double-breasted suit, brightly polished men's shoes, even a fedora and a cane, which she tapped on the floor with each step. She'd painted her face with white makeup, and her eyes were limned with black eyeshadow. She looked like Charlie Chaplin without a mustache.

"Hej, Losman," she said.

Losman, who was unable to speak, simply nodded.

Caroline stood beside him, bringing with her a dense, cloying fog of men's aftershave. She said to the older man, "Have you heard anything about Kramer?"

It took a moment for Jakobsen to gain his wits and respond. "Kramer?" he said. "Who the hell's Kramer?"

"The man who lived here," she said. "The one who died."

Jakobsen stared in fascination at Caroline as if she'd dropped her drawers, squatted, and pooped on his front lawn. "Look," he said, "we were hired to clear this apartment. We don't know anything about who lived here. I'm sorry, but we've got work to do. C'mon, Simon."

Jakobsen started to close the door, but his son stopped it with his arm. "You want us to find out about this Kramer guy?" Simon said to Caroline. Judging by the wide stupid grin on his face, he was clearly smitten by this strange, sexually ambiguous woman before him, and Losman could hardly blame him.

"Could you?" Caroline said. "That'd be so sweet of you."

"No problem!"

Losman stood mute and dumb, until Caroline touched his elbow. "Would you like a coffee, Losman?"

Losman, who had translated only three of his ten pages, didn't hesitate. "Yes," he said. "I'd love to."

Once inside her apartment, Caroline waved Losman over to the couch—a futon the color of a ripe banana—while she went into the galley kitchen off the dining room to prepare the coffee. On her way, she veered into the hall to lean her cane next to her stable of shoes. The apartment was a clutter-free paean to minimalism, with the usual accoutrements Losman by now assumed were requirements in Danish apartments: bare wooden floors, tall windows that offered ample light,

IKEA bookshelves filled with a wide assortment of Danish and English-language books. Losman jerked his head a few times, snorted, puffed air. He knew that if he examined her books closely, he would find Paul Auster's *New York Trilogy* and Tom Kristensen's *Hærværk* among them. Those books decorated the shelves of nearly every university-educated Dane of a certain age that he'd ever met.

Caroline returned bearing a teak tray with a French press, two mugs, a plate of oatmeal raisin cookies, and a small porcelain carafe of milk. She set the tray on the coffee table and sat beside Losman on the futon. He was used to her eccentricity, but he couldn't determine whether this breed of eccentricity was authentic or the phony version of the poseur. Not that it really mattered to him. Either way, he was still attracted to her.

"You really made an impression on that kid," he said. He couldn't believe that he was sitting on Caroline's couch, with Caroline so close that he could touch her knee. Sunlight slanted through the tall living room windows, giving the shadows a hard, linear edge. He wiped his sweaty palms on his jeans. He cleared his throat. He balled and unballed his fist.

She kicked off her shiny men's shoes and removed her black socks—revealing toenails painted in every color of the rainbow—and tucked her legs beneath her. "Did I?" she said.

"You sure did," he said. How could she not have noticed the boy's intense stare and dopey grin? he wondered. Or was she being falsely modest? "He wasn't interested in me once you arrived."

"Was he interested in you?" Caroline smiled, briefly flashing her small, uneven teeth, like a row of tiny pebbles in her mouth. "I'm sorry if I spoiled things for you, Losman."

"You know what I mean."

"I just hope he finds out more about Kramer," she said. "He must've been buried by now. But it'd be nice to reach out to his family."

They sat in silence for a moment. Then Losman cleared his throat and gestured at her outfit. "So, what's the occasion?"

She glanced down at herself as if she'd forgotten her costume. "Oh, I wanted to know what it felt like to dress like a man."

"Like Charlie Chaplin, you mean?"

"I didn't intend to dress like Charlie Chaplin. But once I had the suit on, I realized I could. I already had the hat, cane, and makeup."

Losman nodded as though that made perfect sense. "But why?" he asked.

Caroline leaned forward and pushed down the handle of the French press. She poured two cups of coffee and handed one to Losman. She snatched a cookie from the plate and offered one to Losman, but he declined, and she sat back. "Why dress like a man?" she said. "Like I said, I wanted to know what it felt like." She snapped her teeth into the cookie and began to chew. "And I wondered if it would change me in some fundamental way. Haven't you ever felt like wearing a dress or a skirt, and seeing what it's like to be a woman?"

"Can't say that I have, no."

She swallowed. "You should try it sometime, Losman. You'll feel different."

"I'm sure," Losman said. He sipped his coffee, and he remembered that he had a nearly full cup sitting in his own apartment, cold by now. "Did it work? Do you feel changed?"

Caroline shook her head, disappointed. "Not really. But maybe that's because I'm wearing a bra and panties. A part of me is still feminized. I should remove them."

Losman felt the heat rise to his face. She'd used the word for panties, *trusser*, not the more gender neutral *underbukser*, she'd also used the word *feminiseret,* and he wasn't sure he'd ever heard that one spoken in conversation, but it made perfect sense in this strange context—much like Caroline and her odd behavior made perfect sense. Caroline might be kooky, but there was something very alluring about her and it unnerved Losman to be this close to her. The only other woman who'd ever used the words *bh* (bra) and *trusser* in his presence was Kat, but that had been a long time ago, back when they were still a happy couple. To him, these words were sexually charged, and it felt as though a dormant part of him had begun to stir.

His cell phone began to play a snippet of ABBA's "Dancing Queen," the ring tone he used for his few Swedish contacts.

"One second," he said. He pulled the squawking device from his pocket and held it flat in his palm to read the name on the screen: Lars Andreasson. "Shit."

"Who is it?" Caroline said, tilting her head in concern.

Losman let the call go to voicemail.

"Nobody important," Losman said. He knew what Lars calling meant—that Niels H. must've returned from Corsica and gone to Lars demanding to see pages after Losman had ignored his emails. Exactly what Losman didn't need, now or ever. "I'll call him back later."

Caroline lifted her mug to her lips and drank. She lowered the mug and held it against her chest, cupping it between her palms. Her ice-blue eyes remained locked on Losman, as if daring him to look at her; at any other moment they might hold him in a trance with the mystical power of a hypnotist, but with Petersen's smug face now flashing like a Times Square billboard in his mind, he was unhypnotizable.

"How's the memory study going?" she asked.

Losman balled his hand and squeezed it tightly, forcing himself back to this conversation, thrusting Niels H. out of mind the best he could. How could he explain what he'd experienced on BhMe4 so that she'd believe him? Should he tell her about his Tourette? *Could* he? His mouth was like a cotton ball, so he sipped his coffee, hoping to quench his thirst. But it only made him jittery, even a little sick to his stomach, and he set his cup down. He felt a strange sensation in his chest, like a dozen centipedes skittering under his skin, and now it spread to his belly and groin.

His phone pinged. A voicemail from Lars.

"It's going great," he said, distracted. The director of a major Danish publisher had just left a message on his phone, a message that could set in motion a series of events that could eventually ruin his translation career, turning him into a pauper, and he didn't know what to do. He proceeded to ramble on about FuturePerfect Laboratories, Building 8, the yellow pill, the sensors and beeping machines, and of course his babyhood memories.

"Wait. Are you saying you actually see *memories* from when you were a baby?"

"Yeah. It sounds crazy impossible, I know, but I really do."

"You sure you aren't just dreaming?"

"That's crossed my mind a million times, believe me. But these memories are so specific, and so lucid. It's like I'm right there, alive in them. I can smell my mom's perfume. Taste her milk. I've never had dreams like these before. I'm literally seeing, hearing, and touching things as my babyself."

Caroline's eyes were wide with wonder. She removed her fedora, balanced it on her knee, and ran her fingertip along the brim, as if admiring the gritty texture of the fabric. Her hair today was a dark blue fanned with pink streaks like flamingo wings, a jarring contrast to the Charlie Chaplin costume and the caked-on makeup and eyeshadow. "That sounds incredible. Do they need more people for the study?"

"I'll ask for you," Losman said. He liked the idea of Caroline doing memory therapy with him. It would give them more reason to talk.

"Imagine what it could do for my art? Seeing old memories like that."

He smiled. "You're dedicated."

"I think about my art all the time." She jerked her thumb toward the wall behind her. "When I'm in my studio I'm free to live a rich and authentic life, and I love it. Is that how you feel when you translate?"

Losman shook his head.

"Why not?"

"Translation is just my job. I'd rather be writing my own stories. Then it would feel rich and authentic."

"Do you write fiction?"

"I used to."

"Why don't you now if that's what you want to do?"

"I need to pay bills," he said.

"Can't you do both your job and your art? I do."

He cringed. The answer was yes, he supposed he could do both. But the truth was, his translation work always consumed the bulk of his creative energy and time. First there was the translation itself, which was definitely not easy, then came the second and third and fourth round of his own edits to make the pages respectable and fluid, as smooth and clear as glass. Finally he would submit the book to his editor and begin the next project. Within a few weeks, he'd get the manuscript with the editor's edits and discover that his manuscript was not nearly as smooth as he'd thought, and he'd go through the entire document one edit at a time, cleaning and polishing. Throughout this entire translation and editorial process, he'd have to hustle to find the next book, the next paycheck. Writing fiction was a luxury he couldn't really afford—especially if he lost the Petersen translation.

Caroline said, "The other day I was at Thiemers Magasin, the bookstore over on Tullinsgade, and I found one of your translations in the English-language section."

"You did?"

"Well, *I* didn't. A staff member found it for me. I had to ask her to search your name since I didn't know which books you've translated."

"You looked me up?"

"Yes, I was curious. You've done a lot of books! That's impressive, Losman. But why don't you write your own now? Why wouldn't you make time every day to do what you love to do?"

One flight above, in Kramer's apartment, the saw whirred to life and Losman could feel its vibration in his legs. He welcomed the interruption.

Caroline stood. "Come," she said. "I want to show you my studio."

She trundled down the short hall, beckoning him with her finger. Losman, obeying, followed her into a compact bedroom teeming with paint brushes in old coffee containers, tubes of paint, easels, stacks of canvases leaning against the wall, paint-spattered strips of plastic sheeting, artwork. The curtains were drawn back, and a beautiful orange light filtered into the room, making Caroline's creations seem vivid and alive. The window was open, and the circulating air was gentle and warm. In the center of the room was a large drafting table, on which were a series of charcoal sketches that Losman registered but did not examine. Easels were stationed throughout the room, holding watercolors in various stages of completion, and Losman wandered among them. The paintings had a surprisingly cheerful color palette for lugubrious Caroline, pinks and purples and yellows and reds, calling to his mind Claude Monet and the French Impressionists. Because upon closer inspection, he realized that each represented the apartment building across the street at different hours of the day. The paintings were impressive, he thought, even in a half-formed state. In fact, they were every bit as good as the paintings in her Christiana exhibition.

Losman turned to find Caroline standing before an old-fashioned oak bureau that he must've walked past without noticing, the kind with a broad oval mirror attached to it. "You're a terrific artist," he told her, and instantly regretted his choice of words. He sounded like a proud father, not a potential lover.

"Thank you," she said to him via the reflection in the glass. "It's how I process my experiences, how I make meaning out of my life. By drawing them on paper."

He was struck by how incredibly humble Caroline was, even self-effacing. How could she not see how talented she was?

Casting around for something to talk about, he noticed the sketches on the drafting table, *really* noticed them. He leaned forward and examined the compositions. The first row was a series of black-and-white panels portraying a lonely man seated on a stairwell. The drawings were incomplete, and yet they captured a great deal of raw emotion. Caroline had used the charcoal to outline only the most rudimentary human figure, allowing the white space to represent the man's inner life, which was as bare as the blank page. In simple strokes with an occasional flourish, Losman could see the deep pool of sadness in the man's eyes. The loneliness. The isolation. In one of the panels, he sat slouched against the wall, the picture of abject misery; in another he'd buried his face in his hands, like a father mourning the loss of a child. With a gasp, Losman realized who the man was: Kramer.

He was stunned. Caroline had found a way to imbue Kramer's final night on earth with dignity and humanity and compassion, in spite of the fact that he'd done something hideous. No one who viewed these sketches would ever suspect that this sad old man had drunkenly fallen asleep on the stairwell, pissed his pants, and masturbated in front of Caroline. It was a testament to her ability to empathize with others that she could view him this way, and it made Losman feel very tender toward her. How could she be so forgiving of someone so contemptuous? The truth was, he realized, he didn't know much about her, and this suddenly bothered him. Where was she from? What was her story? How did she become the person that she was?

He easily recognized the second row of panels. They depicted the following day, when the two of them had sat together on the stairwell and Losman had tried to comfort her. He was struck by the evident care she'd taken to sketch him—and that she'd done so at all. One of the sketches showed the two of them holding hands. In her rendering, the conjoined hands seemed to belong to one person; there was no way to distinguish when her body ended and his began. He studied the panel carefully. Was there meaning to be found in those inseparable hands?

"You're so incredible," Losman said. He stared at the hands. Those hands. *Conjoined* hands. Yes, he decided, there was meaning in them. He turned to Caroline. Trembling nervously, he blurted, "Do you want to go out some time? Get dinner maybe?"

8

On Friday night, Losman returned to the FuturePerfect lab in Ballerup. Where he lay in bed now, his body hooked up to all the wires and electrodes that made him feel like a particularly advanced science project, which he supposed he was.

"I want to go to Mrs. Graham's classroom tonight," he said.

Pelin sat on the chair next to the bed, her laptop resting on her knees. She tapped the keys with manic efficiency, then looked up. Her glasses slid down her nose and she pushed them back up with her finger. She blew a particularly mealy snot into a tissue that she clutched in her hand and dropped the Kleenex in the trash bin.

"As I've told you, it's a process," Pelin said, her voice thick and nasally. She looked at him. "Do you really want to skip over several years of your life? Several *formative* years, I might add."

"I want to know what happened that day."

"Be patient, Losman." Pelin closed her laptop and stood. She reached into her lab coat, pulled out the bottle of pills, and uncapped the top. "This may be your journey, but I must insist that we take our time."

Losman stared at the bottle of pills. What was *time?* he thought. With these pills he could go nearly anywhere in his past. His life was not some kid's chapter book with a straightforward, linear narrative. No life was. People march forward from birth to death, but wasn't a lifespan just another plot device? A way to prod our stories to their inevitable conclusion? Along the way there were always coiled knots, loops, and gaps where time seemed to stop or lurch forward. Where detours were taken. Why did Pelin insist on taking him back to the same place every week? "No," he demanded. "This is my story, Pelin. My journey. You just said so."

"Losman—"

"My journey, Pelin. *Mine*. And I want to go to Mrs. Graham's classroom tonight."

"You want to skip five years of crucial memory construction?"

"Why can't I move back and forth in time? I mean, isn't that already what I'm doing when I take these pills? Cheating time?"

"We follow a process that corresponds with your life. What you're asking is to jump an entire section of track."

"It's possible to do that, right?"

"Yes, of course it's possible," Pelin said irritably, as though she were offended at the mere suggestion her pill wasn't a perfectly developed time machine. She sneezed into another tissue and wiped her puffy red nose. "There are two kinds of pills, Losman. I've coded them by dosage. The higher the dosage, the farther back in time your memories will be restored to you. But even if I give you the lower dosage pill, there's no guarantee you'll see the memory you want. A lower dosage simply means that you'll be open to an entire *lifetime* of memories."

"I'll take my chances," Losman said. He flopped back in the bed and pulled the covers up to his chin. "C'mon, Pelin. Let's do it!"

Pelin glared at him sourly. Losman lifted his arms and waggled his fingers in a familiar gesture. Bring the pill over here, it said. In a session two weeks ago, Losman had watched his toddlerself beg his mother to buy him a Tonka truck at Kmart, and she'd eventually given in. This wasn't that much different, he realized. Deep down he was the same little boy, only bigger.

"Fine," she said, "but just this once. Whether you visit Mrs. Graham's classroom or not, next time we go back to our original schedule."

"I can live with that," Losman said.

She upended the bottle on a silver tray and disgorged the yellow pills, which rattled and clinked on the metal like tossed dice. Then she pulled on a purple latex glove and slowly sorted the pills until she found one she wanted. After examining the pill carefully, she typed something into her laptop. "Here," she said.

Losman lifted his hand and Pelin dropped the pill in the center of his palm. He licked his lips. His entire body shivered and pulsed with anticipation. The memory of Mrs. Graham's classroom had been a significant part of his subconscious for as long as he could remember, buried deep like a precious ore. If only he could draw it up to the surface, he would know what actually happened that day, he would understand its true meaning in his life. And now he was about to enter the very shaft where this memory was located. There was a glass of water on the nightstand. Pelin handed it to him, and he popped the pill into his mouth and downed the water. It glided easily down his throat, and he set the empty glass back on the stand.

"Where's Jens?" he asked.

Pelin arranged the duvet, tucking Losman in. "He's already in the control center. Is there anything else you need before I go?"

"No," he said. "I'm ready." Then he remembered Caroline. "Hey, actually. Do you need more participants for this study? I have a friend who may be interested."

"We have enough for the time being," Pelin said.

"That's too bad."

After she'd gone, Losman lay still, listening to Pelin's clicking heels recede down the hallway and waiting for his eyes to adjust to the darkness. He'd learned a few tricks to speed the sleep process along; first, the night before a session, he'd stay up until 4:00 a.m., and he would set the alarm for 6:00 a.m. This week he'd canceled his Thursday appointment with Marlene to focus on revising Niels H. Petersen's novel. When Losman finally called Lars back he'd listened with increasing head-jerking, hand-flexing, throat-clearing anxiety as Lars explained how he wanted Losman to polish up his translation and pass on the clean pages to Niels H. A gesture, he said, of *good will.* Losman had protested, but Lars insisted. *As many pages as you can, okay. That's all.* Once he could no longer stomach revising *I Am Going to Kill You*, he'd run around the lakes so that he would be totally, absolutely wiped out for tonight's session. He was good and tired now.

As his eyes adjusted to the darkness, and the television and the door and the table began to take on vague, blurry shapes, he could feel his body sagging comfortably toward sleep.

But when he closed his eyes to let the Sandman enter, an image appeared unbidden in his mind—a half-formed fantasy of Caroline stepping out of her Charlie Chaplin costume, slowly pealing down to her underwear to reveal her bare buttocks.

"Hello, Losman," called a voice over a loudspeaker, Pelin's. "You'll skew the data with your erection. Whatever you're thinking about, please stop."

At the sound of Pelin's clinically disembodied voice booming into the room, Losman's eyes snapped open, alert and wide awake, his heart pounding. He glanced down at the bulge under the duvet, and instantly—as if reminded of its shameful, unwanted presence—his penis retracted like a turtle into its shell. For a horrible moment Losman feared Pelin and Jens could see into his mind, and he was embarrassed to have his sexual fantasy exposed, until he remembered the electrodes attached to his scalp; the two of them couldn't *see* what was going on in his mind: all they could do was track his body's reactions to stimuli. This made him feel only slightly better.

"Sorry!" he called out.

"Close your eyes, Losman," Jens said in a soothing baritone. "Try to empty your mind."

Losman scanned the darkened corners of the room searching for surveillance cameras, but of course he couldn't see anything. "Are you watching me?" he said.

There was no response.

Losman regretted slipping into a fantasy about Caroline. To his great thrill and relief, she'd said yes to going out with him, though with her surprisingly busy schedule it was difficult for them to coordinate a date. Still, that didn't give him license to reduce her to a sexual object. The subconscious was a funny place, and you never really knew where it would lead you.

He closed his eyes again, and this time Lars Andreasson emerged like a high school teacher scolding him for not getting his homework done. "Send him all you have in one week."

"One week? That's not how I work, Lars."

"It is now."

Stop, Losman thought. *Get those two out of your head.*

He forced himself to start over, this time doing what Pelin suggested, calling up in his mind the scowling image of Mrs. Graham, his fourth-grade teacher, and the day he'd learned that something was wrong with him. The soundtrack of her classroom began to play. *Will you still need me, will you still feed me…?*

BUT HE WENT somewhere else.

He was a small boy, four, maybe five years old. Aksel's age. He was in a warm, comfortable place, in the crook of his mother's arm. In his childhood bed. Staring up, he recognized the glow-in-the-dark stars his parents had taped to the ceiling. His mother lay flat on her back and held an orange and white book over her head. He didn't recognize it at first. She began to read: "Fox. Socks. Box. Knox. Knox in box. Fox in socks."

Fox in Socks! The very words were magical to him, and it was as if a trapdoor opened in his mind, and he fell through. It had been his favorite book. He'd asked his mother to read it so often that, at some point, she'd mysteriously "lost" it. Later, once he'd learned how to read, she'd "found" it and given it to him. He'd spent countless hours reading the book out loud, trying to get through it without making a single mistake, and it had taken him months. Not long after he'd mastered the book, he'd put it aside and forgotten about it. Once it no longer challenged him, he'd lost interest.

He heard his mother's voice low and purring beside him.

He heard his child self laugh at his mother's silly way of reading, and his tiny, tiny voice squealed with delight: *Fox in socks*! Adult him smiled. He didn't *see* the smile, but he sensed it. It was a feeling of joy deep inside him.

His mother set the book aside and kissed his child forehead. She snuggled close to him, nuzzled his cheek with her nose, and said *I love you* in a voice that sounded sweet and young, untarnished by the passage of time.

The child in him felt this love as a powerful, primal force. He felt safe and protected and happy.

Adult him felt much the same thing. It was as if he were in the center of his own being, at the very place where it all began, with no past and no future. Just a wonderful, loving present. Taking this pill *was* a kind of time travel.

If he stayed here, adult him thought, in this place and at this very moment, he would never feel pain again. But of course he couldn't stay. And he *wanted* to feel pain, he *wanted* to taste the humiliation and the shame of what happened to him in Mrs. Graham's classroom.

His vision went to black, as if someone had turned off the lights, closed up shop, gone home. Where was he? He sensed he was somewhere, a kind of wide empty room, but he saw nothing; worse, he *felt* nothing. He was adult consciousness only, a disembodied vessel. He couldn't lift his legs and walk, couldn't feel his way around with his hands.

He was buried alive within his own mind.

"Hello?" His voice echoed as if on the bottom of a canyon. But had he spoken? Or did he imagine it? "Where am I? Pelin? Jens?"

The silence was total. He'd been kidnapped and shoved into a trunk bound with duct tape over his helpless mouth.

He screamed. It filled him, vibrated, bounced, returned, went out again.

And like that, he was somewhere else, shooting through the darkness and into a bright band of white light, and it took him a few seconds to catch up to the shift. But when he did, he felt instant relief. There was a tray, a plate of food, his mother's oval face. She was wearing her plastic eyeglasses that he recognized from photographs taken in the mid-seventies. Her long dark hair, copious and absent a single gray strand, fell to her shoulders and rested there. He watched his chubby little baby arms flail in front of him, knocking against a plate of food and nearly toppling it to the floor.

He was in a highchair, adult him realized.

His mother held a spoon and she brought it to his baby mouth. Something gooey landed on his tongue, tasting of bananas and pears. Baby him spat this goo up and it dribbled down his chin. Adult him felt the tacky, slimy sensation of Gerber's on his face. Baby him blabbered, and adult him tried to laugh but it too came out as blabber.

His mother, he could see, was frustrated. She had dark circles around her eyes as if she hadn't slept in days, and they were red from crying.

Blah, blah, blah.

He spat up again, and baby him laughed seeing his food plop on the white tray.

"Stop it!" his mother screamed at him.

And baby him wailed now, frightened by his mother's anger.

But adult him understood. Now that he had a child of his own, he could hardly blame her.

His mother stood and walked to the kitchen sink, one quivering hand to her forehead. With her back to him, she turned on the tap and splashed water on her face.

And he was transported to another place, one he recognized instantly: his first Christmas in Denmark. Kat's family, the entire Paludan clan—aunts, uncles, parents, cousins—was gathered around the dining table consuming great gobs of roasted duck and pork, red cabbage, potatoes, and rice pudding washed down with Carlsberg and Tuborg and sweet German white wine. Kat's mom piled food on his plate, *you're too skinny* she kept saying, but Losman felt like a dead body washed up on the shore, bloated and unrecognizable. Poke him in the gut and he would explode. Kat was beside him, smelling pleasantly of lavender, her cheeks pinkened from the wine. "What do you like to do?" Kat's grandmother asked him slowly, in Danish. She was a wisp of a woman, pale and haunting even then, six months before her death.

The room fell silent, waiting for his response. Losman battled the feverish urge to violently jerk his head and grunt. He'd been taking Danish classes at the language school, and he was getting better at speaking, but he'd hoped to merge with the wall at this dinner party. Be invisible. "Jeg kan godt lide rejsning," he said softly. It seemed a safe and innocuous thing to say—he liked to travel. A brief and terrible moment of silence followed. Kat's grandmother smiled indulgently, and the room erupted in laughter.

"You like to have erections, huh?" Kat's brother Per said, in English. He winked at his sister. "I bet you do!"

Losman felt the heat rise to his face, searing and intense. He turned to Kat for help.

Kat clutched his hand. She affixed on him a smile so wide and beautiful that it made Losman's heart temporarily seize up—the future Losman, that is, the one seeing the replay of this scene, the one who'd once loved this woman, and probably still did. Her generous smile was etched in his memory. "Du kan godt lide *at rejse*," she gently corrected him.

"Who doesn't love erections, really?" Kat's brother Jørgen said, also in English. "I mean, men, women. There's a little something for everyone—it's like a carnival ride."

"That's enough, Jørgen," Kat's mom said.

Music began to play, filling the entire space above the scene like the score of a movie, and mixed with the commotion of clinking plates and silverware and the lilting rhythm of laughter and the low hum of conversation.

He recognized the tune. *Will you still need me, will you still feed me …*

And now he was in another dark room, but not dark like before. Where? He was on his back, staring at the ceiling. No glow-in-the-dark stars here. But there was plenty of moonglow, a cone of fat, silver light like a bright beacon. Baby him turned his head toward this light but couldn't see through the slats of his … crib. He was in a crib. He heard weeping, his mother was weeping. He listened to her, the tears and sniffling, and the two of them—baby and adult him—wondered what her crying meant. Baby him kicked his legs in the air, grabbing at them with his tiny hands. Rocked from side to side, vibrating his lips and spewing tiny bubbles of spittle.

A light snapped on in the bathroom. Someone was in there. Was it his father? He heard running water splash in the basin, a cabinet open and close, the scrape of the shower curtain.

His mother's weeping grew louder until it became a wail, a torrent of unfiltered and uncontained emotion, and then baby him, sensing his mother's sadness, found himself wailing at the top of his lungs, screeching was the word adult him thought of.

She began to cry harder. Moaning inconsolably. Though he could not see his mother, adult him could picture her sobbing, her shoulders heaving. He understood her frustration. He knew how much energy a child could suck out of you. But what he heard in his mother's sobbing wasn't about him, her child; no, it was something else entirely: it was the dull, drowning pain of unhappiness. Of a hurting soul in need of repair.

Will you still need me, will you still feed me when I'm sixty-four.

"Denise," he heard his father say gently, "what's wrong? How can I help?"

Someone was leaning over the crib, shushing him. It was his mother. No, it wasn't his mother. It was a man in a fedora. No, it wasn't a man, it was a woman. Her face was ghostly white, a mask, but concealed in shadow, and baby him shrieked in terror. Adult him peered at her, eyes squinched in concentration. He'd seen that face before, but where?

Will you still need me, will you still feed me when I'm sixty-four.

"Wake up, Losman," this masked woman was saying. Her mouth was moving, but the words he heard seemed to be coming from some other place. "Wake up!"

LOSMAN BOBBED THROUGH A THICK GELATINOUS GLOOP that slurped and popped in his ears. A sticky film of residue clung to his eyelids, making it difficult for him to open his eyes.

"Losman? Losman, wake up." It was a woman's voice he recognized, but he couldn't place its owner. Between the narrow slits of his eyelids, he saw a strip of light, and instinctively he fought his way toward it. Someone was shaking his shoulder now. "It's time to wake up."

He blinked. His mind was cloudy, a wet, dense fog through which he could not see. Thirty seconds passed, more, and the fog slowly lifted, burned away by the artificial light. The neurons in his brain misfired and he pictured Thomas the Train riding the rails, laughing crazily, *off to work I go, go, go.* Losman's eyelids shot open as if in terror, and he found himself staring directly into Pelin's dark brown eyes.

"Water," he said hoarsely. His parched throat felt like the inside of an oven that had been left on overnight, the pizza inside burned to a crisp. "I need water."

"Fetch him a glass," Pelin said.

Behind her, the lab door opened and Losman watched a blurry figure in blue enter the adjacent bathroom.

"My glasses. Where are my glasses?"

"They're here, Losman." Pelin picked them up from the nightstand and gently slid them onto Losman's nose.

Everything came into focus. "That's better," he said. He tried sitting up in bed, but his head roared with great licking flames of fire. He squeezed his temples. "Oh, oh."

"Do you have a headache?" Pelin asked.

"Yes," Losman whispered.

"Hmm," she said. "That's irregular."

Jens emerged from the bathroom wearing his customary blazer and jeans, his dirty blond hair flopping greasily over his forehead. He handed Losman a tall glass of water. Losman forced himself into a sitting position and chugged the water. It wasn't until he'd finished drinking that he noticed his erection: it held the duvet aloft like a circus pole. He lifted his knees to hide it.

"Why'd you wake me up so early?" he said. "I was just going to Mrs. Graham's classroom. I think."

"*Early?*" Pelin arched her eyebrows. "Losman, you slept for nearly twelve hours."

"Twelve hours? That's impossible!"

Pelin flashed her cell phone for Losman to read the time: 11:07 a.m.

Losman stared at the screen, his mouth open. "How?" he said. A hard punch slugged his brain. "I just went to bed a few minutes ago."

Pelin didn't answer.

Jens set his recorder on the bed. "What did you see, Losman?" he said. "Tell us."

Losman lowered himself onto his back. He closed his eyes and recalled the last image he'd seen. "I saw my mother crying," he said. "And my father was there." A great, terrible sadness welled up in him, which he felt like a heavy weight pushing down on his shoulders. "But something was wrong. Very wrong. I know it. I can still *feel* it. Dad had said, 'Denise, what's wrong?'" He turned to Pelin. "But you woke me up before I could hear her response."

Pelin squeezed his hand.

"What else did you see?" Jens asked.

Grimacing in pain, Losman sat up and pulled at the wires attached to his scalp. "First I want these off," he said.

Jens and Pelin helped him. When they were done, he said, "Do you have any aspirin?"

"We don't here," Jens said, "but I'll get you one."

"Make it two, please."

Jens nodded and left the room.

Pelin sighed. Her face was carved with deep notches that Losman instantly recognized as worry. "Get your clothes on, Losman. Let's get brunch."

LOSMAN WASN'T HUNGRY. He'd wanted to revisit Mrs. Graham's classroom so badly he now felt like a sulky kid who didn't get the birthday present he'd asked for. Out of habit, he poured himself a mug of coffee and toasted two slices of bread, slathering them with thick pats of butter. He'd arranged his erection carefully in his pants, pointing it upward so that he could at least walk somewhat normally, and the awkward bulge would be less noticeable. Still, he'd had to move slowly, like an old man with back pain. By the time he'd made it to the table where Pelin sat with her traditional Danish breakfast of rye bread, a hard-boiled egg nested in a porcelain cup, three slices of cheddar cheese, and steaming coffee, he felt sick to his stomach. Holding his head in his hands, he groaned.

"This headache of yours is disconcerting," Pelin said.

"Tell me about it." Losman's head pulsed like an electrified cable. Before grilling him for ten minutes on what he'd seen in his sleep, Jens had brought Losman the aspirin, but so far, the pills hadn't helped one iota.

Pelin sipped her coffee. She had this way of drinking that Losman would have found amusing on any other day: lifting her pinkie and pooching her lips against the rim of her mug as if she were blowing kisses.

The cafeteria was surprisingly crowded for a Saturday morning. There were between forty and fifty men and women, Losman guessed, all casually dressed in jeans and T-shirts and flip-flops; they looked like sloppy college students the night after a rowdy frat party. A low thrum of constant chatter filled the room on a level frequency, like a radio playing softly. Plates, trays, and silverware clanked on tables and in dish racks. Losman's head throbbed at every noise, and his erect penis poked at his underwear like an unruly pet weasel. Didn't people have better things to do on the weekend than come to work? The cafeteria was a vast hall, bright with natural sunlight pouring through the south-facing wall, which was made entirely of glass. This too made Losman's head hurt. Outside, the sky was a sheet of royal blue, with an occasional tuft of puffy white cloud like in one of Aksel's crude drawings. Beyond the windows he could see a cluster of women walking along the campus sidewalk, talking animatedly with their hands. After a moment, he realized they were speaking in sign language.

Losman watched the women until they were out of sight. He turned to Pelin. "When I was at the Christmas dinner with my ex's family," he said, "it all seemed so vivid, so *real*. It was the realest memory I've had yet. The sights, the sounds, the smells, the uncomfortable feeling of having eaten too much. It was like being there again. Not just remembering the moment but re*living* it. Literally."

"Yes. Revisiting past experiences on BhMe4 often feels that way, especially adult memories. Since they are closer in time, they're much more intact."

"I didn't need the pill to remember that one."

"No," she said. "I'm sure you didn't."

"Why did I go there? I mean, I could go anywhere. How did I end up in *that* memory?"

"Where a subject goes on BhMe4 depends entirely on their subconscious. It's a bit of a crapshoot, Losman. I've said that all along."

The ache in Losman's head was like a hangover, a bruiser of a hangover—the kind you get after a night spent guzzling beer and pounding shots. He stared at his coffee, unable to drink it. "I really wanted to go to Mrs. Graham's classroom," he said.

"I told you there was no guarantee."

"But I was so close, Pelin. I kept hearing 'When I'm Sixty-four.' Even now I hear it."

"You likely experienced what I call an echo."

"What's that?"

"An echo is a repeated occurrence of some element of our lives. Every one of our subjects has experienced it. For one it was a visual cue—a stop sign his father ran. For another, it was the creamy taste of vanilla ice cream on a sunny summer day. When I went on my journey with BhMe4, I kept hearing my grandfather laugh in that deep-throated, genuine way of his that I loved when I was a child. Our brains trap these cues in our subconscious, marking them as important signifiers."

"Of what?"

Pelin shrugged. "A moment in time that is particularly meaningful, for whatever reason."

"That makes sense," Losman said. "I'm pretty sure Mrs. Graham's classroom is *my* moment. I have to try again."

"You'll have to wait for that."

"I don't want to wait."

"You agreed to return to our regular schedule, Losman. You'll get another chance in six weeks."

"I had my fingers crossed, it doesn't count."

"What?" Pelin said, confused.

"Nothing," Losman said, lacking the energy to explain the silly American gimmick. He closed his eyes and recalled the woman in the fedora waking him up. How strange that was. "You know," he said, "my neighbor appeared in my childhood bedroom. It was not a memory."

"You mean your parents' neighbor?"

"No, *my* neighbor. I'm sure it was her. Even my babyself screamed. But could he see her?"

"When did she appear?"

"Just before you woke me up."

Pelin tipped her head back, mouth open. "Well, like I said, you were open to a full range of memories last night. The pill's effect was likely wearing off. Your neighbor could've sneaked in as *a kind of* dream, I suppose. A glitch. But I find it unlikely that your babyself was screaming at her. I believe it must've been a coincidence." She cracked her egg with a tiny spoon and meticulously peeled off the shell fragment by fragment, like an archeological treasure. "The synapses in your adult brain probably crossed wires. No other subject has reported such an occurrence of dream or fantasy merging with memory."

To relieve the pent-up ticcing urge in his brain, Losman wiggled his fingers and squirted a hard puff of air. "But that doesn't explain how my babyself could see her if it's a memory. How do I know the rest of what I saw is real and not a dream or a false memory?"

"We've gone over this, Losman. BhMe4 is designed to locate your lost memories, not produce wild dreams *or* false memories."

"But how can I be certain? I mean *really* certain."

Pelin sighed. She scooped a spoonful of runny yolk into her mouth, chewed, and gobbled up the rest of the egg as though she hadn't eaten for days. Patting her mouth daintily with her napkin, she said, "As I've told you, the sequences you've described to Jens and me are far too lucid to be dreams. Dreams are haphazard, they are scattershot. Images that come and go and blend with your emotional state at the time you sleep. But BhMe4 searches for and finds scenes you've lived and buried deep in your cerebral cortex. Of course, the brain is a complex organ, and we are constantly learning new things about how it functions. We will consider your experience as we continue to develop BhMe4. And I won't reject the possibility of a dream or fantasy meld. I will include it in my notes. What I'm *more* concerned about is this headache of yours—and the fact that it took so long to wake you up. It's not supposed to be that difficult."

Losman recalled how the lights had gone off, leaving him in a black, empty space. He told Pelin.

"That's certainly new," she said. "Did you see yourself?"

"No, not at all."

"What about your babyself? Was he there?"

"I don't think so. I felt completely alone."

"Like a disembodied consciousness?"

"Yeah, that's exactly what it felt like. It was a little scary, to be honest."

"Hmm," Pelin said, pursing her lips tightly. "I don't like the sound of that. That is *very* irregular."

"What do you think it means? The headache? The blackness?"

"I don't know. But I need to feel assured that you're not putting yourself in danger by taking BhMe4."

"How will you do that?"

"I'll analyze the brain scans and the data we accumulated last night, and I'll compare them to previous weeks. If I find a disturbing pattern, we'll have to halt the study."

Losman's eyes grew wide. "You can't do that. I need to know what was wrong with Mom. And I have to get to Mrs. Graham's classroom. I'm *finally* getting close to something really important, Pelin. I can feel it."

"I can't risk putting you in danger, Losman."

"How can you halt it *now*? When I'm this close to making a breakthrough. Isn't that the point of memory therapy?"

Pelin drained her coffee and set her cup down with a hard clink, making Losman flinch. "Let's not jump to any conclusions," she said. "I may find nothing that would endanger you or the study."

Losman nodded, relieved. Well, somewhat relieved. He cleared his throat a few times and leaned back in his seat as far as his erection would allow.

Pelin piled two slices of cheese on rye and took a bite. "Do you think your mother was crying because she had postpartum depression?" she asked.

"I don't know. Maybe," Losman said.

"Why don't you call her? Ask her what she remembers. Memories are like pieces of a puzzle. Now that you're equipped with a few of your earliest, you can assemble the rest of the puzzle by linking them with the memories of others, beginning with those closest to you."

Losman liked this idea. But he also knew his mother. Even if she was able to remember this particular moment, she'd likely just dodge his question. She wasn't the type of person to discuss her medical history with others, especially her son.

Pelin finished her open-faced cheese on rye. "I'm going to get some more coffee," she said, scraping her chair back from the table and rising to her feet. "Do you want anything? Juice? Water?"

Losman shook his head and Pelin headed toward the coffee station at the back of the cafeteria, her tall heels clicking on the linoleum and piercing his brain like daggers. When she was gone, he jerked his head a couple times. Three men and two women already stood waiting for a refill, he noticed. He watched as Pelin got in line behind them. A cafeteria employee wearing a pink smock, her thick hair girdled within a tight-fitting hairnet, removed the carafe and lugged it into the kitchen.

Losman lowered his forehead against the cool surface of the table. What was he doing? he wondered. Why was he putting himself through this? Not once in all the weeks he'd been part of this study had he actually visited a memory that even remotely involved his tics. Had he ever truly believed he would—or could—find *one* definitive answer? Deep down he knew from all the books he'd ever read on Tourette that no one could pinpoint a single causal agent; it wasn't like cancer, where you had malignant cells doctors could identify and say, there they are, let's go get 'em. Taking these pills was like going to a fast-food joint when you were hungry. You skipped the hard part of making a healthy meal for something that was quick and easy but had no nutritional value. In two hours, he'd doubtless be hungry again.

Still, he wasn't ready to give up on BhMe4, because *something* happened whenever he popped those yellow pills. He wanted to return to his crying mother. *No,* he *needed* to return to his crying mother. *Denise, what's wrong? What's wrong?* What did that mean? If he could find out, he would learn something valuable. Something momentous— even if what he learned had nothing at all to do with his tics.

And Mrs. Graham's classroom. That was the Holy Grail of his memories. He had to find his way there.

His eyes landed on Pelin's lab coat. On the pill-bottle-sized bulge in her pocket. A lightbulb flickered in his achy head. Then it switched on. Became an idea. He glanced toward the coffee station to check on Pelin's whereabouts, just as the cafeteria employee returned with a fresh carafe. Pelin was still at the back of the line, she was staring at her cell phone, so Losman had time to spare. He stood and sneaked around the table, doubled over to conceal his erection, watching Pelin the entire time. Once he determined the coast was clear, he fished out the pill bottle. The pills jangled in his hand like a baby's rattle. Loudly. Too loud, he thought, it might give him away. Cupping the bottle and squeezing it tight to muffle the noise, he popped the cap and glanced back at Pelin, who was now second in line and waiting patiently. Looking inside the bottle, he saw that it was filled with twenty or thirty pills, enough that she would never notice any missing. Without hesitation, he upended the bottle and two pills tumbled into his palm; after a moment's consideration, he upended it again and let a third fall. That should be sufficient to get him through the week, he thought, dropping the pills into his breast pocket. He recapped the bottle, slipped it into Pelin's lab coat, and was back in his seat before she returned.

9

AFTER PELIN DROPPED HIM OFF AT HIS APARTMENT, Losman spent two drowsy hours on the couch watching the reboot of *Battlestar Galactica* on Netflix. His head no longer hurt, but he nevertheless felt hungover, and he was twitchy too—his tics like a parasitic fungus that had taken control over his body. Though his erection had mercifully deflated in Pelin's car on the ride home, the rest of his body was now stiff, his joints creaky. He'd tried making a pot of coffee, thinking it would help, but two sips into his first cup his stomach roiled and burbled like an active volcano, and he feared he'd retch if he finished it. So Losman dumped the coffee into the sink, closed the curtains, and settled into his couch to binge-watch the day away.

A little past 3:00 p.m., his cell phone chirped with the birdsong trill he used for Kat. It took him a few frantic moments to locate the phone since it was buried underneath his mountain of dirty laundry.

"Hey," she said. "Can you do me a really *huge* favor?"

From her tone of voice, actually from the very fact of her phone call, Losman knew what Kat wanted. There was only one reason that she'd call him. "I'm not sure I'm up for watching Aksel right now," he said.

"Are you sick?"

"Sort of, yeah."

"Hungover sick or sick-sick?"

"Neither," he said, though he knew what she was driving at. If he was sick-sick she wouldn't ask Losman to sit Aksel, but if he was just hungover, well, that was his own fault, she'd say, and he could buck up and deal with it. If he didn't, she'd make him feel guilty: *He's your son, don't you want to see him? It's not every day you get the chance.* He wondered briefly if he should tell Kat about memory therapy, the pills, and the memories he'd recalled. There were good reasons to do so: A) she knew him better than anyone else on the planet; B) she knew his family; and C) because he was participating in the study for Aksel's sake—which was at least *partly* true—she had skin in the game. But he didn't want to give too much away, either. What if she was critical? What if she told him he was an idiot? Both outcomes were possible, maybe even probable. Kat was determined to move perpetually forward in life, keeping lists of goals she hoped to accomplish by a certain age. She could be hyper-judgmental when the mood struck her, and this seemed like a ripe opportunity. *Why would you look backward?* she might say. *You should look in the direction you're going.* The truth was, he wasn't sure how she'd respond if he told her, knowing that he was popping pills so powerful they tinkered with his brain chemistry. If Losman were being honest, he might even worry about that himself.

"How many hours do you need?"

"Well," Kat said. She paused a beat, sighed dramatically, and went on. "We have tickets to tonight's U2 concert at Parken, and our babysitter just cancelled. I know it's last minute, but I could really, really use your help. If he could spend the night at your place, I'd owe you one."

Losman cleared his throat and jerked his head, just once. Cell phone plastered to his ear, he walked to his balcony and drew the curtains back. It was another gorgeous sunny day, warm and springlike; the sky was so bright that he was temporarily forced to squint. In the building across the street, an elderly woman in a purple bathrobe was fiddling with the laundry rack on her balcony. When he opened his own balcony door, a fresh breeze wafted into the apartment, instantly billowing the curtains, and he sucked a deep, fortifying breath; the air felt good. Vivifying was the word. He'd figured that Kat would be going to this U2 show. She'd been a devout fan of the band ever since she'd first listened to *The Joshua Tree* in school. He'd only become a fan—though fan wasn't exactly the right word—by reason of proximity. Because Kat liked them, Losman liked them. That was the way of relationships, wasn't it? You liked what your partner liked. But once Kat dumped him, he'd gone the other way and avoided them at all costs, since Bono's voice and The Edge's guitar riffs only served to remind him of her. A few years ago, along with millions of other iTunes subscribers, U2's album *Songs of Innocence* suddenly appeared in his account. He'd been so irritated by this so-called gift, which amounted to nothing more than theft of his data storage, that he'd instantly deleted the album without listening to it.

He patted his breast pocket, making sure the three little pills were still there. He'd planned to swallow another tonight and see if he could return to the memory he'd been yanked from when Pelin had woken him up this morning. But it might do him some good to spend the day with Aksel; it would certainly force him out of his head and shake him from this post-pill funk he was in. If Aksel spent the night, he'd have to wait another day to take a pill. He weighed his options.

"Okay," he finally said. His memory would have to wait another day. "Bring him over."

Losman spent the next few minutes picking up his apartment, tossing his dirty clothes in the laundry basket, washing the dishes, organizing his scattered papers and books, making his bed. He even squirted a jet of blue cleansing solution into the toilet and scrubbed until the bowl shined like a trophy.

After he'd tidied up, he hid the three pills in his dresser, well out of Aksel's reach, then stripped and showered. Losman's bathroom was shaped like a long, narrow finger with the toilet at the farthest end, underneath the window. The sink was in the middle, and as skinny as he was, Losman still had to turn sideways to get around it. As was common with so many of these old apartment buildings, there was too little room for an actual shower; you had a curtain next to the toilet, and a showerhead that you held in your hand like a garden hose. And when you were done, you were standing in a puddle that you'd have to squeegee into a drain. Despite the extra effort it took to shower, Losman loved the purifying ritual involved. Closing his eyes like the Buddha, he emptied his mind and let the hot water pelt him at full blast. A good shower— and today was a good shower—cleansed him literally and figuratively.

He felt much better when he was done. He toweled off, scraped the water down the drain, and pulled on a pair of jogging shorts and his Phillies T-shirt.

While he waited for Kat and Aksel to arrive, he guzzled an ice-cold Carlsberg on his balcony, the frosty liquid sloshing down his throat like fuel. On the street below, men and women in shorts and T-shirts walked by his building heading toward Fælledparken, taking full advantage of the beautiful day. Contented, already feeling the calming effect of the beer and the sunlight warming his skin, he smacked his lips and belched. Then he removed his cell phone from his pocket and opened his Facebook app. He checked his notifications and found that he had a friend request from Caroline. Feeling a boost of adrenalin, he immediately accepted. Briefly he visited her wall and noted that she'd recently posted a photo of a gray cat sprawled out on a fluffy pillow within a wedge of bright sunshine. Beneath the photo was a caption, in English, that read: *Don't hate me because I'm meowtiful.* The post had two likes and one smiley face.

He hadn't expected Caroline to be the type of person to post silly cat memes on her Facebook page, but how well did he know her anyway? With his thumb he scrolled down her wall and found that she posted, on average, five to ten times a day. Most of her posts were memes or human-interest articles or videos from *Politiken* or *Information*, about Danish movie stars or actresses or artists. Sometimes she posted an image of her art, with a link to her website, and these drew the greatest number of likes and comments. Anywhere between forty and sixty. Losman was careful not to like any of them for fear she would think he was spying on her wall. He checked her friends' roster and discovered she had only 204. Their only mutual friend was, lo and behold, Katinka Paludan.

Kat.

By the time Kat arrived with Aksel, Losman was feeling pretty darn good. The weather and the beer (he'd had two) and his new Facebook friend had all combined to fill him with a kind of buoyant optimism that had been absent at the start of the day. The recalled memories of his mother ardently crying and his father saying, *Denise, what's wrong?* had been a downer, but now the memory of recalling that memory was no longer forefront in his mind. Which was good.

Aksel strode into the apartment waving his little plastic baseball bat at Losman like the arrogant young regent of a mighty kingdom, his servant Kat following with his overnight bag. The bat had been a gift from Losman's mother last Christmas.

"Hey, buddy!" Losman whooped, high fiving his boy. "What's shakin' bacon?"

Aksel, who had no idea what *shakin' bacon* meant, hopped into Losman's extended arms. "Vi leger baseball i dag!" he shrieked. He was dressed in the red jersey and white shorts of the Danish men's national soccer team, though instead of cleats he wore little boy sandals. His long dirty-blond hair fell down his forehead and into his eyes, and Losman combed through it with his fingers.

Losman hugged him. "Sure, we can play baseball. That's a great idea, buddy."

He couldn't help but smile at his son's interest in baseball, the thing he missed most about life in the United States. This past winter he'd rolled his socks into balls and fastened them with tape to teach Aksel how to swing the bat. And to his delight, Aksel really took to it. Within minutes, he was whapping the sock-ball from the balcony door into the kitchen. Once, he even crushed a frozen rope right past Losman's ear and knocked an empty glass off the counter, shattering it into a dozen shards. Losman had hollered with unfiltered joy. In a matter of days, he'd become Aksel's baseball buddy the same way Losman had been baseball buddies with his dad, and it was glorious. Losman owned a DVD of the 2008 World Series, when his Phillies beat the Rays in 5 games, and Aksel had frequently asked to watch it with him. Seeing the games through his son's mesmerized eyes was like seeing them again for the first time. And Losman had promised Aksel that as soon as the winter was over, he would take him to the park and let him hit.

"You got your wish," Kat said. "A son who loves baseball."

Losman jerked his head and blinked his eyes rapidly, then squirted out a quick snort. Kat didn't know much about baseball, but she was willing to encourage Aksel's interest. "Too bad we don't live in Georgia or Florida or Texas," he said when his body had settled into his post-tic calm.

"Why?" she said, puzzled.

"Because he could play year-round and have a chance to make the big leagues someday."

Kat rolled her eyes.

"All the best players come from those states, Kat. There's never been a single major league player from Denmark. Germany, yes. Denmark, no."

They walked down the stairwell together. On the way, Aksel discovered that if he scraped the fat barrel of his bat against the steps he could generate a lot of noise, which echoed off the chamber-like walls of the five-story building, making conversation virtually impossible. Losman, who carried a bucket of wiffle balls, wondered if Caroline was at home, and if so, what she was doing.

But they met Caroline coming up, balancing her oversized portfolio under her arm. Losman sensed Kat stiffen as she approached.

"Hi," Caroline said without lifting her eyes. She skirted around Aksel and darted past them.

"Hold on a second," Losman told Kat. He trotted back up the stairs. "Caroline," he said.

She paused on the landing. Even in the dim light of the stairwell he could see the red rims around her eyes, as if she'd been crying.

"Are you okay?" he said.

"I'm fine."

"You don't look—"

"What do you want, Losman?"

Losman held up his hands as if in apology, thrown by her unexpectedly curt response. One landing below, Aksel chattered *bah bah bah*. "Are you still interested in memory therapy?" he asked. "They don't have any openings in the study, but I have some pills."

"What do you mean?"

"I mean I took three pills from the lab. Would you like one?"

"You *took* them?"

"Yeah, I'm going to take one tomorrow night. Do you want one?"

Caroline shook her head. "And I don't think you should take one, either. Not by yourself. It's a drug, Losman."

Losman cleared his throat, before balling and un-balling his fist. Embarrassed, he felt like a pusher, an addict trying to ruin an innocent. "I'm sorry. I thought you wanted to try it."

"Not like this," she said.

He returned to Kat and Aksel one landing below. "Nå, what was *that* all about?" Kat said, eyeing him curiously.

"Nothing."

On the street, Kat squatted to kiss and hug Aksel. "You be good for your dad," she said. Aksel wrapped his tiny arms around his mother, and promptly snorted. Squeezing her son tight, Kat looked up at Losman and mouthed, *Don't start*. Then she stood and, to Losman, added, "Thank you so much. I'm grateful for this, I really am."

Losman decided to let Kat's response to Aksel's snort go. She was determined to ignore the problem. Instead, he pointed at the T-shirt Kat was wearing, the one featuring the cover of U2's album *War*: a shirtless, angry-looking boy with fierce eyes. "I know how much you love U2."

She touched Losman's elbow, leaned forward, and actually kissed his cheek. A quick peck. But as her lips grazed his skin, he felt his body tingle. How long had it been since she'd kissed him? Hell, since *anyone* had kissed him.

"What time's the show tonight?" he asked. He nodded with his chin toward the National Stadium. The stadium was within walking distance, and right beside Fælledparken, the enormous green space that served as Copenhagen's closest answer to Central Park. Where he and Aksel were going. "You want to head over with us?"

"No," she said. "Joachim is parked up the street."

"You *drove*? Why?"

"We're staying at my friend Else's place in Brumbleby tonight. We're going to park there and walk over."

Losman hadn't known that Kat had a friend by the name of Else who lived in Brumbleby, and for some reason, this cut him. She'd moved on without him, all right, made other friends. Lived other lives.

He ticced and clutched Aksel's hand as they went down Nordre Frihavnsgade toward the Triangle and the circular BT kiosk. Aksel jabbered on and on, nonsense stuff, and Losman's mind returned to Caroline. He wondered why she'd been crying, and he definitely regretted asking her if she wanted to take a pill. What did she think of him now?

The entrance to Fælledparken was at the corner of Blegdamsvej and Øster Allé. The National Stadium loomed so large on Øster Allé that Losman didn't even have to turn his head to see it, and Brumbleby was right next to the stadium. An old worker's quarter consisting of small, by-now-fashionable row houses, similar to his hometown of

Manayunk, Brumbleby was a popular location to live—if you could find an available place. There weren't many houses to choose from, and once people moved in, they rarely moved out. But if you didn't have tickets to the show and you lived in Brumbleby, you could pull out a lawn chair, sit outside, and hear every single guitar chord or lyric.

Fælledparken was, not surprisingly for such a beautiful day, crowded with people jogging, walking, pushing strollers and prams, playing fetch with their dogs, kicking soccer balls, or throwing frisbees. The sunlight was invigorating, a direct injection of vitamin D into his veins. Although the weather app on his cell phone said it was only 76 degrees, it felt much warmer in the sun, and he saw a few men and women splayed out on the grass sunbathing, desperate to get a little color on their skin after a long, dark Scandinavian winter; most of the women wore shorts and tank tops, but one was actually wearing a yellow two-piece swimsuit. Losman steered Aksel to a free patch of grass close to this woman, who lay flat on her belly reading a book, a shiny gloss of lotion smeared on her legs and buttocks. She glistened like a buttered roll.

Even though he knew it was crass of him, Losman put down his bucket and positioned Aksel in such a way that he could see the woman in the yellow swimsuit read her book fifty feet away. The National Stadium, with its concrete exterior and steel arches, loomed behind him; Rigshospitalet, the National Hospital—where the fictional victims of most of the Danish crime novels he'd read ended their days cooling in the morgue—lay directly ahead. For all its wonderful medical advances and teams of doctors, the National Hospital was just another blocky, square hunk of building that, from this angle, looked like a giant Soviet hotel.

"Ready, kid?"

"Ja!"

Losman wound up and threw the first pitch. It sailed over the imaginary plate and Aksel timed his swing perfectly, centering the barrel of the bat squarely on the ball and poking it with a hollow thwack. "Awesome!" Losman called out.

Aksel got into position for the next pitch, his bat poised over his right shoulder. He squinted at Losman, deep in concentration. Losman threw the ball and once again Aksel struck it hard. *Plunk!* This time it whistled directly at Losman's head, and he snagged it from the air. "Good hit, buddy!"

And so it went. Pitch after pitch, Aksel made contact, and the bucket of wiffle balls slowly emptied. He was a natural, this kid, and Losman observed him with great interest—watching for any sign of tics. But there was none. Aksel's cheeks were glowing with happiness, and he was deeply absorbed in his play. Now that Losman had begun to remember scenes from his babyhood, he wondered if Aksel would remember this day. And if so, for how long? When would the synapses in his brain coalesce enough to store memories? Had they already? The earliest memory he could recall without the aid of BhMe4 had been formed in kindergarten. Though it was fuzzy, and possibly an amalgam of multiple memories, he recalled riding a teeter totter with another boy—whose name and face were lost to him now. Up, down, up down, stomach aflutter.

It made him a little sad to think that Aksel wouldn't remember all the wonderful baby and toddlerhood moments that had made him, Losman, fall in love with his boy. Moments that Losman would remember for the rest of his life—assuming he didn't get Alzheimer's like his dad and lose them—Aksel would have no access to unless some future version of BhMe4 became available to him.

In between pitches, Losman occasionally glanced at the woman in the yellow swimsuit. He hoped she would notice him being a good dad.

But she didn't, of course, and anyway she was off-limits to him, much like Kat and maybe even Caroline were off-limits to him. All the women he was attracted to stood beyond a Maginot line, a perimeter he seemed destined never to cross. What was wrong with him? Why couldn't he find someone? He was in good shape, and reasonably intelligent. He wasn't particularly handsome, but he wasn't ugly either. Didn't he have *some*thing to offer a woman?

He heard a dog bark and he turned to see a chocolate lab hopping around a short, thickly-bearded man in a blue T-shirt on which was emblazoned a hungry Pac-Man gobbling up pink, bug-eyed ghosts. The man held one of those go-fetch-it slings with which you chucked tennis balls; he wound up and let the ball fly, and it sailed through the air as the dog whipped after it with monomaniacal determination. Off in the distance, another man shouted "Nej!" when he couldn't quite reach a frisbee and it fell at his feet.

Just as Losman leaned forward and reached into the bucket for another wiffle ball, a man in a crisp button-down Hawaiian shirt and khaki shorts approached Losman. "This is baseball, right?" he said, in stilted, clumsy English.

"Jeg taler dansk," Losman said, and tossed another pitch to Aksel, who promptly slapped it past him.

"Nå," the man said. "Okay."

"Det gør ikke noget," Losman said. *No big deal,* and it wasn't. Losman was used to people thinking he didn't speak Danish, and considering he was playing an American game with his son and speaking English, he could hardly blame the man. He was much older than Losman, blue-eyed and suntanned, and Losman assumed his grandchildren were off somewhere playing in this park. He was also taller than Losman by several inches, and his bald dome was remarkably shiny, bright as a cue ball. Beneath the dense cluster of red hair on his arms was a universe of freckles. On his feet he wore faded leather Birkenstocks and white socks.

The man stood watching the proceedings with genuine interest, his head swiveling to follow the path of the ball each time Aksel made contact. The next time he spoke to Losman he switched to Danish. "I don't know much about this game," he said, "but your son seems very good at it. How old is he?"

"Three."

The man whistled, impressed, and a sense of pride thumped in Losman's chest. He had a few balls left in his bucket, and now he had an idea. He pulled out his cell phone. "Can you do me a favor?" he asked the man, blinking once, hard, to satisfy a sudden urge to tic. "Can you film my son? I can't do it and pitch at the same time. I've tried."

"Sure," the man said. "Happy to."

Losman handed his cell phone to the man and grabbed the next ball from the bucket. As he prepared to throw, the woman in the yellow bikini reached behind her back and adjusted her bathing suit by inserting one finger underneath the elastic and snapping it out of her butt. It was a sexy maneuver, one that would likely revisit Losman as a lurid fantasy tonight as he lay in bed. But it was not one he wanted in the video. "Wait," he said, putting up his hand to stop the man from filming. "Aksel, move a little to the left, okay?"

The man chuckled. "Smart move. His mom probably wouldn't like that!"

Losman considered telling the man that Aksel's mom wouldn't care one bit, but it wasn't worth the explanation.

Afterward, once Losman and Aksel had collected the balls and returned to his apartment and his Wi-Fi, Losman uploaded the video to Facebook. He was proud of the way his son had launched three consecutive rockets over their heads while the man had filmed, but now that he was friends with Caroline, he was also eager to post something positive. Something she might notice. The last time he'd posted anything on Facebook was weeks ago, and it had gotten one pity like—by his mom. For good measure, he tagged Kat in the post. Even if she didn't understand baseball, she would be thrilled to see how good Aksel was at hitting the wiffle balls.

He set his phone aside and made Aksel mac and cheese for dinner, and as the sun set and the sky turned pinkish orange, they watched *Toy Story 2* in Danish. During the movie Aksel gave an occasional snort—more like a snot-packed sniffle—and even jerked his head a few times. At bedtime, Aksel snuggled close as Losman read Dr. Seuss's *The Butter Battle Book* to him. Aksel was pretty wiped out, and it didn't take him long to fall asleep. Soon he was snoring lightly in Losman's ear, and Losman crawled out of bed and returned to the living room.

He didn't know what to expect when he retrieved his phone and finally checked Facebook. He wasn't a popular person on social media, and his infrequent posts attracted scant attention, five to ten likes *at most*. Through the years he'd somehow added more than 600 people to his friends list, but except for his mother and Kat—whom he hid to avoid all her cheerful posts—he didn't know the majority of them in any meaningful way. They were old friends or embarrassing acquaintances from high school; they were translator colleagues or editors at Danish, American, or UK publishing houses; they were Kat's old friends; and they were random people he'd met here and there. He wasn't the type of person who shared anything of substance. Most of his posts were geeky observations related to grammar: serial comma flubs, comical misspellings, malapropisms. He liked absurdities and dumb shit. Benign, apolitical things that ignited his sense of humor and occasionally connected with one or two language nerds who happened to be online. Once, he pointed out a mistake he'd made on a manuscript that he'd submitted to his editor at one of the big five publishers; he'd misspelled the word "dike" as *dyke* five times throughout the book. That self-deprecating post had garnered more than sixty likes and numerous comments, mostly involving the sticky business of plugging leaky dykes. People liked it when others fessed up to their gaffes.

In terms of active participation, that post had been his best—until today. When Losman pulled up his Facebook app he immediately noticed that he had 10+ notifications. His eyes grew wide in anticipation.

He cleared his throat and shook his head until he felt right. Only three hours had passed since he'd posted the video of Aksel slugging wiffle balls at Fælledparken, and already the post had generated 95 likes and 22 comments. Four people had actually shared it, including Kat and Losman's mother. He didn't know who the other two sharers were, which he thought was kind of weird.

"Little slugger!" his mom wrote. "So proud!"

"Holy shit," a guy who went by the name of Marty McFly wrote. "Little dude can rake!"

Kat's brother Per posted in English, "Time to start soccer!"

Kat posted a heart.

An important literary agent he'd met at Book Expo America in New York City—a man who'd never before liked one of Losman's posts let alone commented—wrote that he should *deeeeefinitely move back to the United States so that kid can ball out.*

Losman laughed, exhilarated. He was overwhelmed by the outpouring of support, and now he sat on his couch to read the comments. When that was done, he clicked to see who'd liked the post, slowly scrolling down the list. It was a strange yet gratifying activity, like zooming through his past in a time machine; so many of the names were people he'd met at various stages of his life, emerging to re-enter his orbit, even if temporarily. The experience left him feeling dizzy, high on some kind of primal giddiness. This is what it must be like, he thought, to be part of a larger community, one where he had dozens of friends and well-wishers. And for the first time, he could truly see why people got addicted to sharing personal photos, stories, and videos on social media. The gratification was instantaneous and intoxicating, and it was as though a deep and powerful bond was forged with every single person who'd connected with his post.

Three-fourths of the way down the list of likes, he found the name that he hadn't realized he'd been looking for until it popped out at him: Caroline Jensen.

She'd *liked* it. Whatever dumb thing he'd done on the stairwell, he hadn't ruined things completely. He still had a chance. His first post as her friend, and she'd liked it, along with 94 other people and counting. Heart pounding, he dropped his phone on the couch and stood up to pace the floor. He was pumped. Caroline could now see that Losman had friends, and he was popular enough to get 95 likes and 22 comments on Facebook. More than *her* typical post.

Already he began plotting his next, because it had to be equally good, it had to generate a large number of comments and likes. Enough for her to notice. Maybe being popular on Facebook might help sway her toward him?

But that, he immediately realized, was fucking stupid. And he was fucking stupid. In his excitement, he'd let himself get carried away to uncharted heights of absurdity. Why the fuck would his Facebook presence sway her toward him? Caroline was an artist, an independent thinker, not a teenager with a crush on a boy. Facebook likes were an illusion, not a barometer of popularity. And anyway, it was one fucking post! If anything, his *son* was the popular one, and as soon as he realized this, Losman felt sick to his stomach. He'd posted a video of an unsuspecting Aksel, he had used his son to score likes and comments on Facebook. How pathetic could a person be?

Miserable now, he returned to the couch and sat down. Only moments before, he'd floated dreamily inside a bubble that had lifted him off the ground. Given him a rare weightless feeling of friendship and camaraderie. But that bubble had burst like a water balloon, and it had splattered all over him, drenching him. He tilted his head back and stared at the ceiling, then juddered with a burst of tics that ran the gamut: jerks, snorts, chuffs, blinks. If he could've cried, he would have.

Never in his life had Losman felt so friendless and alone.

10

LOSMAN SAT ON THE EDGE OF HIS BED staring at the little yellow pills in his palm. When he flipped them over, he discovered to his dismay that each pill had a serial number scored in fine, minute grooves. Two of the pills had the same number, 087651234-H, while the third had a slightly different number, 087651235-I. What did these numbers mean? Did they equal the dosage? Was one pill the pathway to babyhood memories, the other to later memories?

Which one should he take? It wasn't like he could call up Pelin and say, "Hey, I stole some of your pills. Can you tell me what the serial numbers mean?"

When Losman was a boy, he'd read the popular Choose Your Own Adventure novels like everyone else his age. But he never made it far in any of them because his characters were always picking the wrong direction, bluntly ending the story down some dead-end path. It was a pattern that had followed him throughout his life. If given a choice between two directions, Losman always seemed to go the *wrong* way first. With 50/50 odds you had as good a chance of picking the right direction as the wrong one—and yet, somehow, he'd go the wrong way. Was it just dumb luck?

What if he picked the wrong pill and instead of visiting Mrs. Graham's classroom returned to watch his toddlerself learn how to poop on the can again? That wasn't at all what he wanted. What he wanted was the lower dosage pill, the one that could take him to Mrs.

Graham's classroom *and* his crying mother, but which of these pills was the lower dosage? Was there a clue in the numbers? Even if there was a clue, how could Losman know?

This was a serious problem with no solution, and it troubled him. He would have to simply guess, and he didn't like his odds of making the right choice.

With his heart racing, Losman cleared his throat and jerked his head.

In every other way, he was ready. After Kat had picked up Aksel, Losman had jogged three times around the lakes, making himself good and tired. During the sessions at the FuturePerfect lab, he'd always slept through the night, dead to the world. Which meant that if a burglar or murderer entered his apartment while he was off in memoryland, he wouldn't wake up. So he'd made double and triple sure the apartment door was locked. No one was getting in while he slept.

He briefly considered the ramifications of popping the pill on his own, but he dismissed any concerns.

After all, what could go wrong? It wasn't like this was his first time taking BhMe4. By now he was an old pro. In the lab, he was hooked up to a machine, but the machine only read his body's responses to assemble data for Pelin and Jens. He didn't *need* the machine, just a bed and the pill. Sure, he might wake up with a boner and a headache, but eventually they would go away. He would be fine.

What he felt now was a pull, a hard tug. Two nights ago, he'd been this close to learning what felt like a vital truth. The desperation in his father's voice was palpable, *Denise, what's wrong?* And Paul McCartney singing in his ear: *will you still need me, will you still feed me.* Something was there in these memories, he could feel it. Something crucial, and he was on the edge of it. All he needed to do was pick the right pill.

He jerked his head a few times, cleared his throat, and steeled himself to make his decision.

He fingered the pills in his palm, touching each one carefully, as if they might speak to him, tell him *pick me, pick me.* But of course they said nothing, and in the end he scooped up one of the 087651234-Hs and brought it to his mouth. It made sense to pick what he assumed was the most common pill, didn't it?

No, actually it *didn't*. It made the opposite of sense. Pelin and Jens were focused on his baby and toddler memories, age zero to three, and that's mostly what he'd visited the past few weeks. But since he'd taken the babyhood pills in the lab, the common serial numbers were probably those. Right?

Well, maybe. He'd taken three random pills from Pelin's bottle, so he couldn't be completely sure. Go with the one you *don't* think is the right one, he thought, because that means it's probably the right one.

Shit. What ridiculous logic.

Exhaling a long, resigned sigh, Losman put the two 087651234-Hs back in his dresser. There was just no fucking way to know which pill was the right one. He shoved the 087651235-I into his mouth, chasing it down with a glass of water, and lay down on his bed, closing his eyes. Centering his mind, pushing all thoughts aside, he dialed up the two memories he wanted to visit: his crying mother and Mrs. Graham.

He was in a semi-dark room, the only light a soft green glow to his left. As his eyes adjusted to this new situation, Losman noticed his chubby baby hands were raised up in the air before him like a supplicant's, tiny fingers reaching for.... for the baby mobile above. Adult him recognized the mobile for what it was, the solar system: Mercury, Venus, Earth, Mars, Jupiter, Saturn, Uranus, Neptune, and Pluto, back when it was still considered a planet. Driven by their own shifting gravities, the planets slowly tilted from side to side.

He heard the baby in him splutter and squeal and fart, a self-satisfied noise machine delighting in the sounds it produced, and he figured he'd taken the wrong pill after all.

Because he wasn't interested in this moment. This was a random splice of his babyhood with no consequence. Something was different here, too. The light? The air? His baby body? Yes, that was it—his *body* was different. There was no tension in it. No stress. This was one of his happy memories.

But he wasn't looking for happy. Happy wouldn't get him the right answers. How could he jump to another memory?

He puzzled over this question. This was the first time that he'd even considered he *could* steer the ship, actively shift from one memory to the next, like lucid dreaming. But if he'd taken the wrong pill, he could only do so much.

Losman tried to close his eyes, his baby eyes, but could not. When he was in the baby body, the baby was in command. Instead, he focused his adult thoughts on his mother, his mother, his mother, his mother....

And now, suddenly, it was bright daylight. Baby Losman shrieked in laughter. Adult Losman, inside his babyself, saw his vision bobbing up and down. Up and down. Presently he understood why: he was in one of those bounce sets kids have when they're too small to stand. And he seemed to be enjoying himself very much, baby Losman was, yipping and squealing with pleasure. Losman felt this pleasure ripple in waves through his adultself; it made him feel warm and loved and cozy. But as soon as adult Losman understood where he was, he glanced around searching for his mother. What would he find in this memory? Why was he here? Once again, the ripples suggested it was a happy memory.

Which was not what he wanted.

Baby him was barefoot, and his naked toes scratched against a hard, wooden surface. They were on the patio of their new home in Manayunk. There was a smoky grill. The smell of barbecue. There was rock music, Jefferson Airplane's "Somebody to Love." Baby Losman did not recognize the smell or the song, but of course adult Losman did.

Adult Losman knew that baby Losman would soon grow accustomed to his parents' religious devotion to the soundtrack of the 1960s and 70s, but adult Losman had already lived to see this future. There was also a cat named Poobah in this memory, a ginger tabby that had been struck by a car and killed when Losman was six. But here it was very much alive, batting at a golf-ball-sized toy with a tinkling bell inside. Baby Losman watched, mesmerized, as the cat pawed at the ball and hopped after it, mewling.

Baby him bounced, bounced, bounced until adult him felt queasy. His mother sat in a lawn chair reading the *Enquirer*, her face concealed from view, a green bottle of beer in her left hand. A screen door behind Losman screeched open and banged shut, its rusted hinges squealing, and heavy feet stomped onto the deck. Losman felt the vibration in his squat baby legs.

Dad.

But baby Losman was facing the wrong direction. Turn me around, adult Losman thought, turn me around.

This was another happy memory, even if he never got to see his dad. His parents conversed, their voices muffled, unintelligible, as if Losman's ears were clogged. The memory went on and on until Losman's mother gathered him up, lifted her shirt, and crushed baby Losman to her breast. Adult Losman felt his baby lips open wide and latch onto his mother's pinkish-brown nipple. He felt the baby in him suckling and warm, creamy milk flowing into his mouth. To adult Losman, his mother's milk tasted of coffee and Yuengling lager.

Soon his eyes drowsed close.

Then fluttered open. He lay on the couch now, warm piss streaming into his diaper. For baby and adult Losman alike, it felt good, so good to just let it go. He closed his eyes and returned to the joy of unthinking sleep.

Back in his crib now, he heard a noise baby him didn't like. Since he didn't know what it was, it frightened him. The unarticulated language of a baby's emotion sensed dread in the grunts, moans, and squeaky bed coils: Daddy was hurting mommy.

No, no, no, adult Losman thought. I *don't* want to be here. I can't unhear this. This was an anxiety memory. Anxiety memories sucked.

He tried to force his way out, focusing his attention on a memory he'd witnessed at the lab, his crying mother. In his mind's eye he pictured opening up the file, pulling it out of a cabinet..

You put the male part in the female part, he heard his dad say as if from a great distance, far, far in the future. *You do it like this, son. Insert the male part right here. Just stick it in the hole. There. See? Easy peasy.*

No!

The scene shifted, but not to where Losman had hoped. He was now in a highchair, in the kitchen in Manayunk, and his dad was seated beside him, feeding him buttery mashed potatoes with a silver spoon, making airplane noises with each mouthful he pushed toward baby Losman.

"Brrrrrrrrrrrrrrr—incoming! Open up for Air Danny!"

Baby Losman's mouth closed around a spoon laden with food and he was gumming the bland, paste-like substance.

His dad's beard was trim and neatly groomed. No gray yet. He had a full head of hair and those same thick, plastic eyeglasses he would wear for decades. He looked like a graduate student in dentistry. Adult Losman did the math. If he was an infant in this memory, his dad must be twenty-seven—much younger than Losman was now.

His father squinched his face into a parody of a clown. Baby Losman laughed, spewing a hunk of food on his high-chair tray. A fucking happy memory again.

"Oh, look what I've done," his dad said in mock seriousness, wiping baby Losman's mouth with a paper towel. Adult Losman felt the force of his father's hand scrape against his chin and, in spite of himself, delighted in the touch. His father was a whole person again, his mind sharp and *there*. Young. Still relatively fit and muscular. What a gift, adult Losman thought, a bonus.

I love you, Dad, he said. But, of course, his father couldn't hear him.

And now they were playing catch in the local park. Losman saw the baseball coming right directly at his face and in the very last instant the glove went up and caught the ball and Losman was throwing it back to his waiting dad, who snatched it out of the air and tossed it back. Again and again and again. His dad wore a plain white T-shirt, cut-off jean shorts, and a Phillies cap. This memory was a few years later, and his father had a beer belly now, a soft, round lump like a partially deflated basketball, but he must've been in his mid-thirties. Still the strong, vital man Losman had adored as a boy. The version he remembered the best, active and happy and a little goofy.

He'd picked the right pill after all, he thought, momentarily disoriented, but his rare triumph didn't last. In the very next instant he was dumped into a blackness so sudden and total he feared he'd gone blind. He was bodyless now, floating in an empty space as vast as a universe or as tiny as a pinhead, he didn't know which. Entombed, that's the word that came to him. And he screamed in terror.

Time passed—how much Losman wasn't sure.

"Hello!?" he called out, his adult voice a disembodied echo like before. He felt for his arms and legs and face, but found he had no arms, legs, or face. "Hello!!?"

No babyself.

Absolute silence. Deathlike stillness.

A streak of red lightning flashed through the blackness, sizzling and popping like fire before vanishing. A moment later, another. And then another. And then another. Until the blackness around him was luminous with thin, sinewy forks of crackling, blood-red lightning.

And then, jarringly, he was thrust into his babyself again, wrapped in his father's strong arms, going up and down. Loud music blared from an 8-track player, Led Zeppelin's "Tangerine."

It was his childhood bedroom in Manayunk. And oh was it a relief to see.

His father was painting the wall with a thick brush smeared with navy-blue paint. Losman's toddler hands reached into his line of vision and rested on his father's much larger hand, and Losman could feel the tiny hairs on his father's fingers.

"Are you helping out, buddy?"

The smell was acrid, harsh—and adult Losman suddenly recalled this smell. This *stench*. How it had lingered for years in his bedroom, faint but ever-present. He'd slept in it, played in it, lived in it. Hated it. Now he watched helplessly as his father splattered it on his walls.

His father began to sing along with Robert Plant, off-key, tone deaf, right in baby Losman's ear.

And the scene shifted once more. His father was gone, and he, Losman, was walking down the street with a teenaged Aksel, a bright, sunny day in Copenhagen and the two were headed to the park. Aksel was tall and slender now, gangly, with long, scraggly hair and an Adam's apple. Acne pitted. He carried a baseball bat and a glove, Losman a bucket of wiffle balls. They found an empty patch of grass beside a woman in a yellow bikini. When Losman set the bucket down, she turned and looked up at him, but her face was cracked and fragmented, like shattered glass.

How was this possible? he wondered. *How*? This was no memory. This was the future. Or, no, it was some sort of fantasy mixed with his memory of yesterday.

Why was he here? In this place? Something was missing too, he sensed, something essential. Something he couldn't name. He was moving his feet, he was walking, but he had no volition. He was not in control of his own body. He was hovering above it, observing the scene as if from the height of a drone, in a soundless vacuum, a surreal silence.

The woman in the yellow bikini faded like a ghost and vanished.

Clouds formed, gray-black and immense, and scurried across the darkening sky. It began to rain. Buildings rose up like thousand-eyed monsters, fell away. Colors dripped, and Copenhagen melted into a runny black smudge.

Losman watched himself reach out to Aksel, dropping his hand on the boy's knobby shoulder. But when Aksel turned around, it was not Aksel—it was himself, it was Losman—and he realized what was missing in this fantasy: his babyself.

His babyself was gone, and Losman was sitting on a riser in Mrs. Graham's classroom surrounded by his classmates, but their faces were as fragmented as the woman in the yellow bikini's had been, as though some kind of acid had been spilled on this memory and it had been contaminated, destroyed. But his classmates weren't important to him, Losman thought, only Mrs. Graham. And her face was not distorted. It looked exactly as he remembered. She was seated on a chair before her students. A short, plump woman with thin, dark hair and skin like bleached stone, she was wearing a simple black skirt matched with a blue blouse, a colorful silk shawl, and hoop earrings.

"Ladies and germs!" she announced like the ringmaster of a circus. Her voice was surprisingly brassy, deeper than Losman recalled. She placed a record on the turntable and dropped the needle carefully. "Please listen to the brilliance of this song."

The needle scratched the record, and the familiar trio of clarinets formed the intro to "When I'm 64" and Paul McCartney was singing the first verse.

Losman had done it. He'd found the memory. He was here. Finally, he would find out what had happened. But even this triumph was short-lived, because in that very same moment he noticed something truly horrifying. He was in his adult body, and he was completely, undeniably, one-hundred thousand percent certifiably naked and erect.

And he was instantly propelled through a thick, smoky haze toward a circle of white light.

LOSMAN CAME TO, ON HIS KNEES, NAKED. Slowly and groggily, he emerged into the bright, effervescent light of consciousness. A few moments later, Losman saw a hand—undeniably his own—diddling with his penis, whapping it back and forth like a toy. Without his eyeglasses, Losman's vision was bleary, unfocused. He tried to squint but could not.

What the fuck? Was he awake, he wondered, or still inside a memory?

Laughter emerged from his throat, but it was not *his* laughter. It was the small, mousey laughter of a delighted child, a toddler.

Where am I? What's happening?

The laughter, louder this time, more hysterical. The insistent bark of a seal.

Losman saw the floor getting closer, his body somehow moving on its own, his erection like the dial of a compass guiding the way. He was crawling on his knees now, feeling no pain, no sensation whatsoever, pulling at the box of toy trains, tipping it over, spilling its contents with a clatter. He watched his hands aimlessly push a stack of tracks. What was happening to him? How were his hands moving?

And Losman realized, to his horror, that he was awake and inside the mind of his babyself, who was now in charge. The pill had worked in reverse. Rather than his adultself entering his babyself to retrieve his memories, his babyself had entered his adultself and overtaken his body. Losman could see through his own nearsighted eyes, but he was incapable of acting or moving his own limbs. His body had become a toy, like Optimus Prime, one of Aksel's Transformers, and Losman was simply a tiny passenger within its skull.

Fuck.

His hands tossed the tracks aside, and Losman's giggling babyself returned to his penis. When the erection suddenly deflated, becoming as flaccid as a cooked noodle, it was a small mercy.

But this mercy only seemed to confuse the toddler, spurring him to acts of aggression. Something was wrong with his toy. With the toddler in charge, Losman's body shifted its hips, and his soft penis waggled from right to left, left to right. The toddler clutched the penis with Losman's hand and slapped it back and forth.

How long have I been in here? When did I climb out of bed? When did I remove my clothes? He couldn't recall anything of the morning; it was like having a blackout following a night of excessive drinking. Judging by the light in the apartment, a bright boxy square entering from the east and casting its wide net on the couch and the dining table, it definitely was morning.

Losman focused every ounce of energy on influencing the toddler in charge. *Get up. Find my glasses. Put some clothes on for god's sake.*

Get out of my body.

Let me be me.

But influencing the toddler in charge was like eating tomato soup with chopsticks.

What if I'm stuck like this forever?

Losman wanted to cry. He should have listened to Pelin; he shouldn't have stolen her pills.

Sound emerged from his mouth, an indecipherable blabber, the approximation of human speech. Losman recognized it as the nonsense sounds a baby makes when it's learning language.

Losman was still on his knees, the toddler inside him was still diddling with his penis, when there was a knock on the door.

Trapped like a prisoner inside his own head, all Losman could do was watch. A blur of movement, his naked body squatting on his haunches, blabbering babytalk. Crawling forward.

Toward the door.

No. Please no. Don't go to that door!

But he was not in control, the toddler was. Blurting gibberish, the toddler pulled and yanked and prodded at the handle. From deep within the kid's muffled brain, as if far down the end of a long, spacious hallway, Losman heard a woman's voice on the other side of the door, unintelligible. *Lo...n? Lome?*

Somehow—as if accidentally—the toddler unclicked the latch and whoever was in the hall slowly inched it open.

When Losman saw who it was, even in a blurry, unfocused form, he wanted to crawl into a cave and die. He wanted to put a gun in his mouth and pull the trigger. He wanted to leap out the window to his death. He wanted a nuclear explosion to destroy the world. He wanted to be anywhere, *anywhere*, but right here, right now, inside the head of his naked body. Literally helpless as a baby. Taking that pill had been a terrible, terrible blunder, and he would pay for this blunder for the rest of his life as surely as his name was Daniel P. Losman. Beginning now. From behind the veil, Losman watched as Caroline slowly took form in the doorway. She wore a flouncy blue summer dress patterned with what appeared to Losman's poor eyes to be yellow daisies. Perched like a huge bird on her head was an enormous, wide-brimmed sun hat, which, when coupled with her silky white, elbow-length gloves, made her look like one of those fashionable women who dudded up to watch the Kentucky Derby. A small, slender rope of hair, dyed purple, poked out from underneath the brim. She was barefoot, and her toenails were painted a plum-purple to match her hair.

The toddler in charge was captivated by this new thing in the room, a big-hatted woman with purple hair and toenails.

After the split-second it took Caroline to fully absorb the elemental fact of Losman's spectacular nakedness, she reared a step back, stifling a scream with her hand.

"Oh my God," Caroline said, eyes bulging from their sockets. "Losman? What are you *doing*?"

In response, the toddler in him shrieked with delight. *Yeeeeeee!*

"*Losman?* What's the matter with you?"

The toddler in charge blathered babytalk. Caroline stood frozen in place, her eyes darting from Losman to the stairwell, from danger to safety. Fight or flight.

I'm not going to hurt you! Losman screamed. But of course she couldn't hear him.

Losman's arms shot up as if to say, Pick me up! Pick me up!

Caroline retreated until her back was jammed against the door frame and she couldn't go any farther. She peered into the hallway and seemed poised to run, to escape this bizarre spectacle, when the toddler in charge of Losman's body suddenly tipped him to the floor and began to bawl. *Whaaaaaaaaaa.*

"Losman, my God. What is *wrong* with you?"

I'm in here! Help me.

He blacked out. Returned to that vast dark space with its streaking red forks. The sky—if you could call it that—filled with an aurora borealis of glowing light. Explosions of bright red dots, splashes of ink, networks of lines. That sizzling sound like frying bacon. Losman saw this like in a dream. From within this pulsing glow, a plush toy with huge eyes stared at Losman, its stumpy arms and legs lacking hands and feet. Solly! Though it had no mouth to speak, Losman heard it plainly say in a child's pleading, trusting voice, "Up! Up!"

He was thrust into a new memory, into a new *consciousness*, one that shivered and pulsed and tried desperately to expel him. Something gripped him and began to thrash him about. Like being in a mosh pit at a heavy metal concert, he felt he was being pushed and shoved by many hands at once. He was standing at his 8th grade locker next to Alicia Adams, the cute blond he'd crushed on until she was a sophomore and moved away. Horrified, Adult Losman recognized the scene, and he wanted to back out immediately, but he was forced to watch.

"Hi," Alicia said, giving his younger self a cute little wave.

Young Losman could not speak to Alicia, could not even look at her. He rummaged pointlessly in his locker—for what? His books? Adult Losman was overwhelmed by the raging emotions inside his gawky adolescent self, the heart-pounding fear and crippling anxiety, and felt like he was on fire, burning up from within.

"Are you going to the dance on Friday?" Alicia said. Losman was surprised to hear her deep Long Island accent, the way the 'a' in dance stretched like a piece of chewed bubblegum. Had he noticed that back in school? He remembered, vaguely, that she'd moved to his district in 5th or 6th grade, but at that age he wasn't particularly interested in dialects. Young Losman dared a quick glance in Alicia's direction, allowing adult Losman to see that she was wearing a turtleneck sweater patterned with bright red squares across her chest. Her enormous hair was spiked up high with what must've been an entire can of ozone-depleting hairspray, and she smelled of Baby Soft perfume. Adult Losman felt an incredibly powerful urge to touch Alicia's ostrich poof of hair, to crunch it down beneath his hand until his fingers were sticky. Alicia glanced back at the three girls who'd made Losman's life a constant churn of humiliation throughout middle and high school—Jenny Woods, Amy Potter, and Stephanie Torrance—and because his younger self wouldn't let him fully enter his consciousness, adult Losman saw what his younger self never did: the smile. The girls' stifled giggles. This was a trick, a dare, and poor Losman was the target.

"Maybe," his younger self managed to say. "You?"

"I am. Do you want to go with me?"

"*Me?*"

"Uh huh. Do you want to go with me?"

"Okay. Yeah. Sure!"

"I know you do," Alicia said, ramping up to deliver the line that would haunt Losman for months. First she blinked rapidly and jerked her head, mocking him without mercy. "But there's no way I'd go with *you*, Blinky."

She spun on her heels and returned to her cluster of friends, who roared with laughter and high fived her. "Oh, my God," he heard Amy Potter say. "I can't believe you actually did it!"

Adolescent Losman leaned his forehead against his cool metal locker and crumpled inside, and adult Losman felt the hot tears brimming in his eyes. A teacher emerged from her classroom, Mrs. Johnson, and gently touched Losman's shoulder. "Losman?" she said. "Can you hear me, Losman?"

"Can you hear me, Losman?" Caroline said. Losman's eyelids slowly parted, and he saw Caroline's blurry face hovering inches from his, her hand lightly tapping his cheek. She spoke to him like a mother to her feverish child. "Losman, I don't know what's happened to you, but you've got to wake up."

The toddler in charge babbled his response.

Jesus, Jesus, Jesus. He's still in there.

Caroline stood up and moved out of the toddler's sight. A moment later she returned with a T-shirt, shorts, and a pair of tighty-whities. She dropped the garments on the floor one by one. "You need to put something on before Kat arrives, Losman."

At this the toddler mewled like a giant baby.

Kat's coming?

Because Losman's body was dead weight, Caroline had to roll him back and forth to pull his underwear on, grunting from the strain. The toddler made no effort to help. A bead of sweat formed on Caroline's forehead, and her face flushed crimson. Once his underwear was on, she paused to take a breath before repeating the process with his shorts, until Losman looked like a man ready for a nice brisk jog on a beautiful spring day.

Caroline looked him over. She said, slowly, as though he were deaf or dumb or both, "Kat will be here any minute. Do you understand?"

There was a series of loud knocks on the door, three hard claps. Even through the muffle in his ears, Losman could hear them. He groaned, knowing that it was Kat and fearing her fury. *Why the fuck would you do this to yourself?* he imagined her yelling. He would have no answer. A moment later, Kat entered in a flurry of movement. As if on cue, Losman's lips made butterfly noises and he began to blabber.

Jesus fucking Christ.

"How long as he been like this?" Kat asked Caroline, staring down at him on the floor as if from a great height, her face a blur.

"I don't know. He was like this when I arrived."

Kat squatted and put her hand on his forehead. "He doesn't feel hot."

"I don't think it's a fever. He's just acting—really strange."

"Losman," Kat said. "Losman, can you hear me?"

I can hear you!

"He's not responsive," Caroline said. "Shouldn't we call an ambulance?"

No! Don't call an ambulance! Call Pelin! Look in the drawer!

Losman's hand tugged at his crotch, and Kat pulled it away.

"He's been doing that a lot," Caroline said. "I can't make him stop."

Kat pursed her lips in a tight, thin line, the way she did when she was chewing on a particularly meaty question. She cupped his chin and turned his head this way and that. Leaning forward, she lowered her face to Losman's, close enough that he could see the fuzzy blond down of her facial hair, and gently lifted his eyelids. It was as if he were sitting in a command tower and this giant fifty-foot-woman was putting her eyeball directly up to the glass and peering inside—as if she *knew* he was in there.

To Caroline, she said, "His pupils are dilated. Did you notice that?"

Caroline came forward and leaned in next to Kat. With their heads side by side, they appeared to Losman like blue-eyed conjoined twins, though one had a bright streak of purple hair. He babbled and drooled.

"Losman," Kat said. "Are you on *drugs?*"

You could say that.

Caroline said, "He told me the other day that he'd taken some pills from this memory therapy he was part of."

"The fucking idiot!" Kat hissed in English. She walked away and returned a few moments later holding what Losman recognized as a business card: Pelin's. She must've found it on his desk. He'd forgotten about that card, and seeing it now jolted him with relief.

The toddler had begun to whimper. It was now hungry.

Caroline stuck her finger in Losman's mouth, and the toddler began to suckle, making the wet, squishy, satisfied sounds of a nursing child.

Great. Just great.

Kat took out her cell phone and punched in Pelin's number. She jammed the cell to her ear and began pacing the floor out of Losman's view.

Pelin must've answered her phone right away, because Losman suddenly heard Kat's raised voice punctuated by moments of silence.

"What the fuck is wrong with him?"

…

"He's acting like a baby!"

…

"How am I supposed to know?"

…

"What do the pills look like?"

…

"What color did you say? Yellow?"

…

Losman's toddler mouth continued to suckle on Caroline's finger.

"I found them," Kat said. "Two yellow pills with BhMe4 inscribed on them. Is that what you mean? Yes? Okay. You have to do something."

…

"How long will you be?"

Kat hung up. She stood over Losman. "You *stole* her pills? What the hell were you thinking?"

I don't know.

"Look at you. Jesus Christ." She took a deep breath and turned to Caroline. She exhaled. "I'm sorry, but I have to go. If I stay here any longer, I'm going to explode. This Pelin woman will be here in fifteen minutes. She says she'll take him to their lab. Can you stay with him until she arrives?"

"Yes."

"Thank you," Kat said, sounding both relieved and exasperated. She stormed out of Losman's apartment, slamming the door behind her.

I'm really sorry, Kat. I didn't mean for this to happen.

"Well," Caroline said to him, "I guess you're hungry. Let's get you something to eat." She found Losman's eyeglasses on his nightstand. "Are you in there, Losman? Do you need your glasses?"

Yes, please.

With some difficulty, she helped him to his feet and guided him clumsily to his small dining table. She rummaged in his drawers until she found one of Aksel's bibs and put it on him. From the fridge she withdrew a carton of yoghurt and scooped the yoghurt into a ceramic bowl with a spoon. She sat down beside Losman, dipped the spoon into the bowl, and scraped up a blob of yoghurt. "You know what's funny?" she said. "I spend a lot of time imaging myself as someone else, getting dressed up, pretending. And here you actually are someone else. A baby. What's it like?"

Caroline held Losman's chin steady and inserted the spoon into his mouth. "I know you can't talk, so I'm going to do it for you. I wonder if you'll remember what happened to you when you return to normal." She paused to give Losman a look of grave concern. "I hope you return to normal, Losman."

You and me both.

Caroline peered into his face with her cool blue eyes. "My ex-boyfriend used to like it when I wore costumes," she said. "It turned him on. I didn't dress up for him, I did it for myself, but I let him believe it. It was easier that way."

The toddler spat a hunk of yoghurt from Losman's mouth and laughed hysterically.

"I want to find myself, Losman," Caroline said, patiently wiping his mouth and chin with a tea towel, "but I also want to be someone else. Do you know what that's like? To be stretched in two directions at once?"

I know exactly what it's like.

"You're really a piece of work right now, Losman, you know that?"

She lay the soiled tea towel down on the table. "I grew up on the west coast of Jutland, on the North Sea, about as far away from Copenhagen as you can get. I hated it there, Losman. Hated it. I was desperate to leave." She paused to scoop another spoonful of yoghurt. "I can't ever live there again. It would kill me. My brother is the assistant branch manager of the Brugsen in my hometown. Working at a grocery store is a practical occupation, my parents say, because people need to eat. You'll always have a job, they tell me, you can't make any money drawing measly portraits. That's what my parents think I draw. Measly portraits. When are you going to get a real job? they ask. They don't accept me for who I am and it's demoralizing. Their attitude is like a poisonous worm in my brain, constantly feeding and drizzling its toxins, and thanks to this worm, sometimes I think they're right. I am worthless, I will never amount to anything. That's why I dress up like others, Losman: I want to *be* someone else. You probably don't know what that's like."

I do, Caroline! Trust me, I do.

Caroline went on in this vein for several minutes, and Losman was startled by her high degree of self-loathing. He listened as the toddler whined.

"When I was ten," she said as she was changing his shirt, which was now lumpy with thick white splotches of yoghurt, "my family rented a cottage in Skagen. You know Skagen, right? The beautiful port town famous for its light and its beaches? When the tide is low there, temporary islands form. Sandbars. They are very pretty, but also really dangerous because the North Sea, Skagerrak, and the Kattegat all collide there. Well, that summer a German tourist swam out to one of these sandbars about a kilometer from shore. Before long the tide rolled in and cut him off from the mainland, trapping him. The waters raged all around him, crashing into one another, and slowly ate up his island. Within minutes he'd drowned. There was nothing he could do. He'd watched his island shrink, knowing that he was going to die.

"I cried and cried, Losman, until my mother took me back to the cottage where we were staying. To this day, she thinks I was crying because the man drowned. It was very sad, it really was, and I don't mean to make light of his death, which was awful, but I wasn't crying for him, Losman. I was crying because even at age ten I understood the symbolism in his death. I was afraid *I* would drown if I stayed in West Jutland.

"I don't know how many times I've painted this man since. Someday I will show you my collection."

I want to go with you to Skagen, Caroline, I want to see your collection.

By the time Pelin arrived—with Jens in tow—Caroline had fed Losman, cleaned his face, and changed his shirt. Like a mother preparing her son for a school trip, she'd even packed his Phillies duffel as an overnight bag with a change of clothes, his toiletries, and a snack.

Jens shoved his hand under Losman's armpit and guided him slowly down the stairwell, ramming the full force of his bulk against Losman's body. Since Losman couldn't offer any help, it was slow going, and he could hear Jens's muffled panting heavy in his ear; a big man who was clearly more comfortable in a library than a gym, his face turned the color of a freshly harvested peach from the exertion. Pelin and Caroline followed closely behind, helping whenever necessary to keep Losman's body balanced and stable on his feet. Once they'd finally reached the sidewalk, a passerby gawked at Losman as he toddled toward the open car door, mouth open, drooling like someone who'd had a stroke.

Fuck off!

Jens carefully lowered him onto the backseat and Losman slid down on his side, limp as a doll. Pelin climbed in the back with him and sat on the edge of the seat. From the medical kit at her feet, she withdrew a syringe as long as a butter knife. The last thing Losman saw before his eyelids closed was the look of severe disappointment on Pelin's face as she jabbed the needle into his thigh.

Part III

Losman is Alive

11

LOSMAN AWOKE IN WHAT WAS BY NOW A FAMILIAR PLACE, the antiseptically clean bed in the FuturePerfect lab in Ballerup, his hand clutching an invisible object that he somehow understood was Solly. Bright LED lights checkerboarded the ceiling panels like the UFO in *Close Encounters of the Third Kind*. What the fuck happened? With all the electrical doodads in this windowless room—the flashing red terminals and monitors, the enormous TV screen, the peeping machines—he felt like he was in the underground lair of some wealthy computer geek who was building a secret corner of the dark web. Even so, he was relieved to be here. Out of the toddler's mind. He lifted his hand and waggled his fingers. He opened his mouth and made a noise, a loud ahhhhhhhhh. He blinked, licked his lips. When he jerked his head a few times and snorted, his tics returning with a spiteful vengeance, he knew for certain that the toddler in charge was no longer running the show. He was back to his old self.

Holy shit.

Turning his attention toward the nightstand now, he saw through his fuzzy vision a ham sandwich packaged in Cellophane and a bottle of Apollinaris seltzer. His eyeglasses were there too, and he put them on. That's when he noticed the small white card leaned against the bottle, the word *Velbekomme!* written in a fine, loopy script in blue ink.

Losman, who was famished, propped himself up on his elbows. As he reached for the sandwich, the two wires attached to his scalp fell between his eyes. One by one he plucked them off and tossed them over the side of the bed. Quickly he unwrapped the sandwich and wolfed it down. As he chewed the dry, tasteless food, he made several significant observations: 1) He did not have an erection. 2) He did not have a headache. 3) He was alone in the lab, though 4) he had likely alerted Jens and Pelin that he was awake by removing the wires from his head.

5) How the fuck did he get here?

6) Caroline had seen him naked and acting like a baby. So had Kat. *Fuck, Fuck, and Fuck.*

He finished the sandwich, then unscrewed the cap on the bottle and gulped the fizzy citrus-flavored drink. When he was done, he belched, screwed the cap back on, and returned the empty bottle to the nightstand. He climbed out of bed and discovered he was still wearing tighty-whities. Somewhere in the room, a machine beeped, a solitary *doot* like the alarm clock on a watch.

There was a knock on the door. Before Losman had the chance to respond, the door opened and in filed Pelin and Jens.

"Christ!" Losman said in English, yanking the duvet from the bed and covering himself. He jerked his head twice and snorted. "A little privacy, please?"

"It's nothing we haven't seen before, Losman," Pelin said. She wore a powder-blue lab coat over a black skirt and white blouse, and block-heel slingback shoes with thin leather straps secured around her ankle. Was this considered business casual? Losman wasn't sure. Her long brown hair was piled in a messy bun atop her head, and her stylish, blue-framed eyeglasses now dangled against her chest on a red cord.

Pelin and Jens scraped two white chairs over to the bed and sat down. Jens placed his recorder on Losman's bed without bothering to ask for permission; he opened his notebook and clicked his pen. Pelin motioned with her hand for Losman to sit, but since there were no other chairs in the lab, Losman crawled back into the bed and drew the duvet up to his chin.

"I'm very, very disappointed in you," Pelin said in the scolding tone of a mother. "Why did you steal the pills?"

"I didn't want to wait another week."

"You could've permanently damaged your brain," Jens said. He was dressed in his typical uniform of blue jeans and blue blazer and slick patent-leather brown shoes, but there was something different about him today, Losman noted: his customary white button-down, untucked, appeared to be made of expensive silk. His loose, jowly cheeks were ruddier than usual, swarthy even, as if he'd been called to the lab during a date night with his spouse, one bottle of house Merlot into dinner.

"I'm aware of that," Losman said. He pointed to his head. "It was scary being stuck in here."

"You're very lucky," Pelin said.

"*Lucky*? I made a complete ass of myself." Losman grimaced as he recalled being a toddler in front of Caroline and Kat. What he felt now was no different than waking up after a rugged bout of heavy drinking to gradually piece together all the foolish shit he'd done while inebriated. "I don't need BhMe4 to remember that."

"Yes, Losman, lucky. Very much so. That pill could've warped your brain forever."

"They're your pills, Pelin. You're the one who developed them."

"That may be true, but I also told you I had concerns. I was running tests. I didn't encourage you to take them on your own. In fact, I believe I was pretty clear about the importance of taking the pills in a *controlled* environment and following our instructions. It's even in the intake agreement you signed."

Feeling tense, Losman jerked his head and grunted. He glanced up at the giant TV and noticed his reflection on the dark screen staring back at him. He knew Pelin was right. "Look, I'm not going to argue with you. I shouldn't have stolen your pills. I *was* afraid I'd be stuck like that forever."

"I wasn't sure if you'd *ever* get out. You were asleep for sixteen hours."

"Sixteen hours? Jesus," Losman said. "Does that mean it's Monday?"

"Yes. Your body was detoxing."

Holy shit, he thought. He'd wasted an entire day—two, really, since his prime translating hours were now. He was already behind schedule. He had to revise those pages! How many days until he had to send them to Niels H.? He couldn't remember. His clothes were heaped on the floor. Feeling suddenly anxious to get back to his work, his body seized with a rare full-body tic—arms, hands, head jerking like he'd been electrocuted. He crawled out of bed and began to get dressed.

Jens said, "Not to mention the danger you put *us* in. Do you realize the liability we're talking here?" He shook his head disapprovingly at Losman, who was zipping up his pants. "We have a hell of a mess to clean up thanks to you."

"I'm sorry about that," Losman said. He really was sorry, too. He tugged a T-shirt over his head and heard that solitary *doot* again. He wasn't sure what it was, or what it meant, but Jens and Pelin didn't seem bothered by it, so he let it go. "I didn't expect—"

Pelin said, "You're not a scientist, Losman. You weren't analyzing the data like we were. Listen." She paused to regard him. "You can't take the pill anymore."

"Don't worry. I don't *want* to take it anymore. I've had my fill."

Losman grabbed his socks and sat on the edge of the bed, drooping his head in embarrassment and shame. An urge to chuff air through his nose overtook him. He'd screwed up everything lately. Just when he'd begun to make inroads with Caroline, she'd seen him tootling around naked as a mole rat. How could she look at him in a romantic way after that?

Jens leaned forward in his chair and rested his elbows on his knees, the ballpoint pen in his hand tightly wedged between two thick, furry fingers and poised over his spiralbound notebook. "What memories did you see when you took the pills?" he asked. "We might as well discuss them."

Losman turned to Pelin as if for confirmation that this was in fact a good idea. When she opened her palm as if to say, *Go ahead, might as well*, he began to put on his socks. With all the excitement, and horror, of the past 40 hours, he hadn't given a single thought to the most recent memories he'd located deep in his brain.

"I'm not sure what I saw, to be honest," he said, reaching for his sneakers and clearing his throat. "I mean, this was a weird trip."

"Tell us," Jens said. "Go on."

Losman cleared his throat three more times and jerked his head twice. He hooked his sneaker with his index finger and let it dangle there. He didn't know quite where to begin. His memories crowded in, shoving and bumping into one another, demanding his attention like filthy, greedy children. He closed his eyes and tried to think logically, which to him meant chronologically. Unlike with his dreams, his memories always arrived fully intact. All he had to do was begin talking. They gushed out now, a steady stream. Recounting each memory, he was amazed at their voluminous depth, how he could recall even the tiniest of details.

He narrated his film roll of memories, and in the process, he lost track of time. As he talked, Jens scribbled furiously in his notebook. A court stenographer with a ballpoint pen. At some point, Losman realized he was directing his stream of words solely to him, or more specifically to his recorder and notebook. As though his words were meant for something much larger than all of them combined. He stared at the little black recorder catching his every word. He was addressing some future scientist or historian who'd unravel the vast mystery, make everything clear. When he was finally done, Losman felt a singular tightness in his chest, like a man who'd just sprinted up a steep hill and was short of breath.

"What do you think?" Pelin asked Jens. She'd been silent during Losman's monologue, legs crossed, hands resting on her thigh.

Jens held up one finger to finish writing his notes. After he was done, he closed his notebook and laid it on his lap. "I find it very, very interesting," he told her. His ruddy cheeks, stippled with a topography of tiny blue veins, gleamed like an apple. He turned to Losman. "What do *you* think?"

"What do *I* think? I'm not the professional, Jens. You are."

"I'd like to hear your interpretation."

Losman scowled and rubbed the nape of his neck. "When I took the pill the other night, here in the lab I mean, I'd thought something was wrong with my mother, or with me. I'd hoped to get back to that moment to figure out what it was, but I didn't. I didn't learn *any*thing with these latest memories. Not one thing." He could feel the stiffness in the ropy cords of his shoulder muscles, so he rolled his head from side to side to get the kinks out. "But you know how I told you things went completely black the other night? Well, it happened again, only this time the blackness lasted longer. I mean a real long time. It was strange as hell. And when I was stuck inside the toddler, I relived an adolescent memory I never wanted to see again."

Jens opened his notebook again, his eyes widening in anticipation. He leaned forward. "Go on," he said. "We're listening."

PELIN WALKED HIM TO THE BUS STOP. When they entered Building 8's grand foyer, six stories of steel beams girdling brick and glass and wood, the blinding natural light forced Losman to squint until his eyes adjusted. Three layers of gently babbling water cascaded down a ten-foot-tall fountain that resembled an elaborate wedding cake, incongruously placed on top of which was a bronze statue of Venus de Milo. He hadn't paid much attention to this statue before, and now he wondered why it was there; it didn't fit with the modern architecture or décor. In the bright shaft of sunlight, the fountain's clear water sparkled like pixie dust, and a small, misty rainbow rose like a mirage from within the spray.

Losman followed Pelin through the igloo-shaped tunnel and outside. Into another warm, sunny morning. The beautifully manicured campus grounds spread out before them like a lush paradise, carpeted with thousands of inky, purple crocuses, and he sucked in the clean air. They were the only ones around, and together they walked down a pebbled path bordered by cherry trees bursting with bright pink blossoms. Birds twittered and danced in the branches as if drunk on sunshine. The cloudless blue sky shone with the translucent shimmer of a tranquil sea. The day was so transcendent, so paradisiacal, that he half-expected to see a fat, loping grizzly bear happily giving a small boy a ride on its back. Over the years, Losman had entertained a number of Jehovah's Witnesses in his apartment. He wasn't interested in their religion, but if he was feeling lonely, he would listen to their spiel. At the end of every visit, invariably, they would hand him their literature, copies of *Awake!* and *The Watchtower.* And after they'd gone, he'd flip through the pamphlets and chuckle at the images he found in them: lions and tigers frolicking with lambs and children; adults flashing ivory-white teeth in broad, orgiastic smiles; cornucopias of fruits and vegetables and healthy foods free of high-fructose corn syrup and trans fats. This campus today reminded him of those idyllic scenes. He jerked his head.

They ascended a small rise and from there they could see down the slope, where the yellow bus was already idling at the stop, as if patiently waiting for Losman to arrive.

"It leaves in ten minutes," Pelin said, lifting her eyeglasses from where they dangled on her chest and putting them on to read her smartwatch.

They started down the slope, their shoes crunching on the pea gravel. They could see the bus driver behind the wheel reading *Jyllands-Posten.* Losman, feeling guilty, cleared his throat and said, "I'm really sorry about stealing your pills and fucking everything up. I obviously didn't think things through."

Pelin didn't respond, and Losman understood why. There was nothing for her to say. Losman had jeopardized her research, her life's work. No apology could undo what he'd done. He'd put himself in a dumb situation by taking that pill on his own, but now that he was free of the crazy, dick-pulling toddler, he felt he'd been given a second chance. Somehow, he had to make things right with Caroline—and Kat.

He said, "Will I have flashbacks? Could my babyself slip back into my body?"

"That's unlikely," Pelin said. She hesitated. "But we'll have to monitor you to be sure. If you feel anything strange call me immediately." She plucked a crocus from the grass and held it under her nose, breathing deeply. "Tell me, Losman, has memory therapy helped you?"

"All it's done is turn me inside out."

"What about the memories you've seen? Do you at least feel closer to the heart of yourself? Your tics?"

They reached the stop, and Losman fished his cell phone from his pocket. He glanced at the driver, a man with dreadlocks spiraling like tight coils from his head, and seized up in a brief but forceful series of tics.

"Not really," he said, when the fit passed. "But I certainly have interesting new memories." He'd come close to some kind of truth, perhaps, but close was as far as he was going to get. He was done taking BhMe4. Another question nagged at him now. "Why would I see my son as a teenager if BhMe4 recalls *memories*?"

A squirrel dashed up a tree, and Pelin watched it scamper along. "BhMe4 acts on something called the default mode network," she said. "The default mode network is the region of the brain that allows us to call up our memories or imagine the future. Perhaps you tapped into something that wasn't really a memory. Until you came along, I wouldn't have thought it possible. But now, with this new data you've given us, I will have to recalibrate."

"Then it *was* a fantasy and not a dream? Why was Copenhagen melting? And why was I naked in Mrs. Graham's classroom?"

"I don't know, Losman, but you did not see dreams. Not in the strictest sense of that word anyway. As I told you—"

"I know, I know," Losman sighed. "BhME4 doesn't call up dreams."

Pelin gave his shoulder an awkward pat. "Anyway, Losman, the interpretation of fantasies is beyond my area of interest or knowledge. Can I give you a piece of advice?"

"Sure," Losman said. He steeled himself for a lecture, one he no doubt deserved.

"During our time together you've been focused solely on reliving bad memories," Pelin said, "as if it was only in them you could find out what's *wrong* with you. But what if there isn't anything wrong with you, beyond the fact that you're simply human, trying to make your way? Getting by in life is hard enough even on the best of days. It's okay to make mistakes, it's okay to not be perfect. Stop focusing on unhappy memories, Losman. Find a way to make *new* memories. Happy memories. Isn't that what life is about?"

Losman frowned. "Aren't you the ones who told me I could get to the bottom of my Tourette with this pill? How else was I going to do that?"

"Yes," Pelin said. "We did tell you that." She gazed off into the middle distance at the golden field of wheat beyond the bus stop. "But maybe that was a mistake."

12

LOSMAN DIDN'T GET BACK TO HIS APARTMENT until shortly after 11:00 a.m. His cell phone was on the dining table. There was a message from Kat, *text me when you get home.* He typed a response, *I'm home,* and pushed send. He set the phone down and brewed a pot of coffee, sat at his desk, and opened his document. Do something, his OCD brain told him, get some work done. A bright patch of sunlight poured into his apartment, falling squarely on his computer's display, scorching his eyes. His tics were out in full force—head jerks, air chuffs, snorts, shoulder rolls—stoked like flames by his anxiety. To distract his mind and get started, he put on soft, low music, Pachelbel's *Canon in D Major.* But this old trick didn't work; the words swam before his eyes. The day was lost.

He checked his phone. No response from Kat.

He stared at his computer screen and scrolled through the draft. Before today, he'd already revised the first 58 pages to his relative satisfaction. There was a murder and a body, and Niels P. had started the investigation that would, eventually, loop back to his pathetic self. All the little telegraphed clues that pointed like flashing neon road signs to the moment when Niels P. began his murderous spree. Drivel. It was all fucking drivel, and the thought of spending more time on it made him want to gag. Drinking his hot coffee, he felt his body warming up, his brain getting clearer, and he decided he'd do something for himself for a change, to hell with this bullshit translation. He would travel to the island of Ærø, like he'd always wanted, and spend a couple days there. Why not? He needed a break.

He copy/pasted the first 58 pages into a second document and sent it to Petersen (cc'ing Andreasson) with an unapologetically brief note: *Here's your sample.*

He opened his web browser and began looking for places to stay, finding a quaint cottage in the town of Ærøskøbing that only cost $38 a night, and he booked it, surprised at how easy it was for him to spend money on something that two or three days ago would've seemed frivolous, a luxury he couldn't afford. He opened a new browser and bought round trip train tickets. More expenses. His train departed from Copenhagen Central at 1:30. He'd have to take the bus to Østerport and then the Metro downtown.

Kat arrived as he was jamming three days' worth of clothes into his backpack, announcing her presence with two efficient raps on the door. He stuffed his Moleskin notebook and a novel—*Oryx and Crake*—in his pack and set it down in the hallway, took a deep breath, and let her in.

"What the hell, Losman?" she said, brushing past him in a blur of movement. Her familiar scent of lavender perfume trailed her like a gassy cloud. She strode over to his couch and plopped down. "What were you on yesterday?"

Losman closed his door with a soft click. He cleared his throat and jerked his head a few times. "BhMe4."

"What the hell is that?"

Losman cracked open the acronym like a hardboiled egg and explained it to her. "It's a pill that returns your babyhood memories to you," he said.

"You're kidding, right?"

"Nope. Believe it or not, it works."

"Works? How? By turning you into a babbling idiot?"

Losman sat in his reading chair. He jerked his head and cleared his throat.

"Do you even *remember* yesterday?"

"Yes and no."

Kat stared at him, her eyes like laser beams. She wore blue trousers and low-heeled shoes, also blue, with a white blouse. Around her neck she'd wrapped a multi-hued scarf swirled with clots of primary colors, a messy painter's palette; her thick blond hair fell to her shoulders like strands of corn silk, and two smooth blue opals the size of nickels dangled from her earlobes. She must've dashed straight here from work.

Kat noticed his backpack propped against the wall like a giant stuffed bear with four stubby flaps for legs. "Where are you going?" she asked.

"Ærø," he said. "For a few days."

"You can't run from this, Losman."

"I'm not *running* from anything, Kat. I just need to get away."

She glared at him. But Losman didn't flinch. He wasn't going to let her make him feel small, not this time.

"Coffee?" he asked. "It's fresh."

"No," she said. "Yes."

"Which is it?"

"Yes."

Losman went to the kitchen and poured Kat a mug. As he did so, he gazed through the window down at the rear courtyard. A man and a woman were on the playground with a small boy, a toddler younger than Aksel. The father lifted the boy up and set him carefully on the slide, let him go, and the laughing mother caught him at the bottom. Losman recalled how, only the day before, he'd been a toddler himself. Again. And he cringed at the memory of flopping around unashamedly naked in front of Caroline. He dumped a spoonful of sugar and a dollop of milk into Kat's coffee, the way she liked it, and returned to the living room. He handed the mug to her, and she set it down on the coffee table.

"Why would you take this drug?" she said.

Losman didn't answer right away. During the years they were together, they had discussed his Tourette on countless occasions, and he didn't care to have this conversation with her yet again. He'd always tried to hide his tics and vocalizations from people, but in withholding this part of himself he'd also become a bit of a recluse who struggled to find meaningful or lasting relationships. Or keep the ones he had. Kat had never understood why he didn't come out of his shell more often, try harder—why he always seemed to ghost people he cared about. What she never understood was how difficult it was for him to feel worthy of another's friendship or love. How he always feared they'd learn the truth about him and turn away, abandoning him like his friends inevitably did, one by one, when he was in elementary school. Like she had, eventually. That kind of hurt he couldn't bear, and anyway, hiding his tics was much easier when he was alone.

"I wanted to get to the bottom of my Tourette," he said.

Kat snorted as if she'd expected something like this. "You and your Tourette," she said.

He explained at great length what Pelin had told him, taking pains to recall as many details as he could. It was important for him that Kat understood why he'd participated in memory therapy, despite the risks involved. "I did it for Aksel as much as for me. I don't want him to live with this, Kat. If I can get to the root of my condition through my memories, maybe I can help Aksel too."

Kat listened in what appeared to be a state of ever-increasing agitation. She set her jaw tight and stared at him. When he was finally done, she said, "Okay, sure. The pill helps you see your earliest memories, I get it. As crazy as that sounds, I get that part. But what I still *don't* get is how taking this pill helps you understand your tics? And how in the world is it supposed to help Aksel? He's only three. He could just be copying you. You ever think of that?"

Losman jerked his head. He knew it would take some work to convince Kat. "Pelin—she's the woman behind the study—"

"I know who she is," Kat said. "I talked to her, remember?"

"Right," he said, clearing his throat. "Well, Pelin's theory is that buried somewhere in my childhood memories is a clue."

"A clue to what?"

"An environmental factor that set off a genetic determinant and caused my Tourette."

Kat laughed. "Those aren't your words, Losman. They sound like something grown wild in your brain, an invasive species that's crowding out your *own* thoughts."

"What does it matter if they're my words or not?"

"Listen to you, Mr. Translator."

"That's not fair, Kat."

"Okay, fine. I'll play along. Let's say they're your words, how do you prove such a thing?"

"I don't know. I never quite understood that part, to be honest, but did you know there's an actual gene that may cause Tourette? And it can be *edited*. I mean," Losman fell silent a moment, letting his head droop. "Maybe someday it can."

Kat pursed her lips tighter. Losman recognized this maneuver—the tighter the line the greater her irritation. Toward the end of their relationship, he had seen plenty of this pinched-face look, and he always considered it the calm before the storm. "You don't *know*?" she said. "You put yourself in danger and you don't even know how it works?"

"I know how it sounds, Kat. But I'm telling you, the pill worked. I have memories now that I didn't before."

"And yesterday you were a baby, Losman. A *baby*. Do you think that's normal?"

"That was my mistake. I wasn't supposed to take the pill again so soon. Or alone."

Kat picked up her mug and lifted it to her nose, sniffing the coffee as though she were afraid Losman had emptied a vial of the yellow pills into it. She took a perfunctory sip, grimaced, and returned the mug to the coaster on the coffee table. He always made strong, dark coffee, which Kat, who liked it weak, always seemed to forget. "How do you know they're memories anyway and not some hallucinogenic trip?"

"I've wondered that myself. I mean, it's weird to think you can actually see these old memories—"

"Give me an example of what you saw."

Losman ran his hand through his hair, chuffing air.

"Out with it, Losman." Kat glanced at her watch. "I don't have all day."

"Fine," he said. He downed his by now lukewarm coffee, girding himself for what was to come. He cleared his throat and told her how he'd seen his mother and father when they were still young, and even Poobah, the cat who'd died when Losman was six years old. The cat he'd completely forgotten about! He told her his favorite memories, the ones that were most babylike—riding in a pram, his circumcision, even breastfeeding. As he spoke, his voice rose two or three notches, and he realized he was pleading with her. Trying to force her to believe him. When at last he finished, he sank into his seat, breathless.

Kat was silent. She squinted at him, her face transformed; the tight lines were gone, the disapproving edges, replaced by something softer, sadder. As if she felt badly for him for being such a credulous dumbass. He dropped his head into his hands and stared at the floor, anticipating her laughter. Now that he'd retold his memories to someone he'd known for years, someone he loved, even now, he had to admit they sounded asinine. And yet, he'd seen them play out, he'd lived them. *Re*lived them, actually.

After he was done, he blinked convulsively and made a clicking noise with his tongue.

"I guess that explains why you always liked sucking on my nipples," Kat said. "You must've been subconsciously remembering your mother's tits."

"Fuck off," Losman hissed. He went out to his balcony and stood with his hands on the railing, watching the cars zip by on Nordre Frihavnsgade, buttery smooth, midday sunlight flashing on polished chrome, blinding winks of light. A car honked at a jaywalking man. The A1 pulled up to the bus stop and came to a halt, its brakes shrieking. A light breeze caressed Losman's skin. Kat joined him at the railing. He still hadn't brought his patio furniture out of his basement storage unit, but at this moment he wished he had.

"I'm sorry, Losman." Kat rested her hand gently on his shoulder. "That was mean of me. I'm just trying to comprehend all this."

Losman shrugged free of her hand and went back inside. He stared at his computer. Kat stood next to the couch, watching him.

"Are you going to be all right, Losman?"

"I'll be fine. I just need to get away from here."

Kat turned to go.

Losman sat down. "I hate these tics, Kat," he said, "how they control my life. I'd do anything to make them go away."

Kat paused at the door. "What if it's all in your head, Losman?"

"You think I'm making this up, Kat? You of all people? You lived with me for thirteen fucking years!"

"No," she said. "I don't mean that your tics are in your head. I mean that you give them too much negative energy. You're your own worst enemy. They control your life because you let them."

"That's easy for you to say, Kat. You don't know what it's like."

"You're right, I don't, but that doesn't make what I'm telling you any less true."

Losman gave her a dismissive wave. "Go, please."

Kat said, "I still care about you, you know. I want you to feel better."

"You have a funny way of showing it."

Losman redirected his focus to his computer. He knew he was being petulant and unfair, but at this moment he didn't want to look at Kat, and he certainly didn't want her to tell him how to live. She had no right, not anymore. Negative energy. Fuck that. One by one he closed the open tabs. In the deliberately slow amount of time it took him to accomplish this task, he sensed her eyeing him, knowing that she expected him to look up, to turn, to say something pleasant. To end on a good note. Like a good boy. Like a good Losman. But today was different, and he had nothing more to say to her. When he heard the soft click of the door closing, he was glad.

But Caroline was another matter. What would she say to him? How would she react? How in the world do you have a normal conversation with a woman after what he'd done? What he deserved was a hard slap to the face.

He hoisted his pack onto his shoulders and locked the door behind him. Then he made the slow, difficult journey up one flight of stairs to Caroline's place, and after taking a deep, calming breath, he knocked.

No response. He planted his ear against the door, listening for the telltale creak of a wooden floor, the approach of a 105-pound woman in her bare feet. Or, at the very least, a blaring stereo or television set—something, anything, to indicate her presence. But there was only empty silence. He drummed his fist harder.

A moment later, Losman gave up and turned to go; she was not home, or she was avoiding him. He'd been worried about seeing Caroline today, wondering how she'd respond to him, but as he trundled down the stairwell to exit the building—bouncing on the balls of his feet, his big pack throwing him off balance—he realized that *not* seeing her today was much, much worse. Because it meant that at least three days would pass before he'd have an opportunity to apologize for his behavior, and how would that look to her? Would she think he was avoiding her? Instead of seeing him once again as a responsible adult, one who could own up to his mistakes, would she continue to see him as a blathering toddler obsessed with his own dick? Worse, would his absence solidify that image in her mind? The thought made him recoil in embarrassment.

But what could he do? He had a bus to catch, and a train, and a ferry—all of which were regulated by strict schedules. If he missed just one, he'd be forced to wait for the next, thus screwing up the entire trip, and he'd risk losing even more money. Although he didn't mind spending a little on himself, he still had to be careful.

Once outside, he turned to the left and the right, hoping to spot Caroline on the sidewalk. Maybe she'd gone to the bakery? Or the gym? But no such luck. He waited for a cluster of bicyclists to pass before hustling across Nordre Frihavnsgade to the bus stop. Already he could feel the sweat forming a broad, tacky band on his back, from his shoulder to his tailbone, so he shrugged off his pack and propped it on the pavement. He sat next to an old woman wearing a blue paisley dress, who ignored him, her jaw clenched in a stony grimace. He glanced up toward Caroline's apartment on the third floor, wondering if he'd see her standing at the window, but he did not. When the bus arrived, he scanned the faces of everyone who disembarked. After the old woman boarded, he followed her on and schlepped his backpack to the center of the crowded bus. He shoved his pack under one of the luggage racks and stood for the entire ride to Østerport station. Though it was a short trip, the stop-and-go traffic jostled him back and forth, and by the time he got off he felt sick to his stomach.

At Østerport he plugged his earbuds into his ears and listened to all 11 minutes and 25 seconds of Bob Dylan's "Desolation Row" while waiting on the platform. With the sun beaming directly on him, he felt swaddled in a suffocating blanket, and was grateful for the cool air the train offered when it finally shuttled him downtown.

Copenhagen Central was teeming with people when Losman arrived. He strolled through the vast concourse with the distracted air of a tourist with time to kill, dodging a passel of Japanese families

clumped near the information booth. At one of the many shops in the
bustling hall he purchased a bottle of water, a banana, a newspaper, and
his favorite Danish pastry, a *tebirkes*. Losman devoured the fatty hunk
of sugar and butter covered in poppy seeds as he watched an aggressive
pigeon prance undisturbed in search of food scraps among hundreds
of moving human feet, its head bobbing as though it were attached to
its neck by a loose spring.

AS THE TRAIN CHUGGED TOWARD ODENSE, the city of Hans Christian
Andersen's birth, Losman consumed his newspaper, engrossed, high on
the rediscovered joy of reading simply for pleasure. He didn't bother
to suppress his tics. Periodically, he'd glance up from *Information* to
stare out the window at the low, rolling hills patterned in wide squares
of wheat and corn, and the vast, gorgeous fields of yellow rapeseed
illuminated—like a van Gogh painting—by the brilliant circle of sun
in the diaphanous sky. How long had it been since he'd ventured this
far from Copenhagen? Since he'd luxuriated in the beauty that was the
Danish countryside?

In Odense, Losman changed trains and headed south toward
Svendborg, where the ferry to Ærøskøbing would depart. It was a
42-minute trip with stops in Årslev, Ringe, and Kværndrup. At Svendborg,
the last stop on the island of Funen, Losman filed off the train along with
everyone else. In the station, he picked up a glossy tri-fold brochure of
things to do on Ærø and made the short walk to the port. There he stood
on the pier. In the distance, way out on the Svendborg Sound, he could
see the Ærø ferry like a tiny blue dot on the horizon.

The breeze on the pier was refreshing and cool, but the air was thick
with the tangy smell of brine and fish. Feeling meditative, Losman
closed his eyes and let the warm sunshine bake his skin, and he listened
to the water lap against the big stone breakers. There were hundreds
of gulls out on the water; he heard them screech and watched them

dip and dive and soar. To his left, a long line of idling cars was queued up waiting to board the ferry. To his right, a father and son stood with fishing poles braced in their hands, buckets at their feet. Losman recalled bank-fishing as a boy with his father at his grandparents' place on the Susquehanna River. The names of the fish they'd caught still dazzled him: walleye, trout, black crappie, bluegill, smallmouth bass, channel catfish, northern pike. He watched the father and son fish, thinking of Aksel and how he'd like to share such an experience with him. The son was a blond, apple-cheeked boy of eight or nine in soccer shorts and a windbreaker, while the father had a thick beard and wore a heavy woolen sweater and white cap. He smoked a pipe, and the burning tobacco made its way into Losman's nostrils. Losman had always appreciated the scent of a good pipe, and he soaked this in, too.

When the 4:05 ferry finally arrived, he clambered aboard, making his way to the lounge deck. After the boat embarked on its voyage to Ærøskøbing, its massive engines brumming like a great beast raised from a deep slumber, Losman went upstairs to stand outside on the viewing deck.

With the fierce winds of the open water rushing against him, Losman watched Svendborg shrink as the ferry lurched farther into the sound, the orange terracotta tiles of its cityscape gleaming in the sunlight, the pyramid-shaped spire of Vor Frue Kirke piercing the sheer web of blue sky. Under the churn of the rotors, the ferry cleaved through the water, like a zipper. Losman watched the sailboats, miniature white specks a few nautical miles away, skim across the surface as swiftly as bugs.

BhMe4 was a kind of oracle, he thought. But maybe the past, like the future revealed in the oracle, was best left unknown and undisturbed? His journey on the pill had taught him at least one thing: there was no single memory buried deep within his brain that would reveal his innermost truth to him. Memories weren't like the plot of a crime novel, where a murder is committed and clues are dispersed like a trail of breadcrumbs, leading to the killer. To a neatly wrapped-up story like in *I Am Going to Kill You*. They didn't form a discernible pattern at all, in fact. Memories were far more complicated than that.

The ferry set its course between the small islands of Skarø, Drejø, and Hjortø, keeping the larger islands of Funen and Tåsinge within sight, and as it drew closer to its destination, Losman felt a glorious serenity wash over him, as though he'd descended into a dark pit but somehow escaped to tell the tale. And soon he would arrive on the island of Ærø, the one place in Denmark he'd always longed to visit. He snapped photos of the islands as they passed, and he posted the best one on Facebook, regretting it immediately. Why should he announce his movements to the world? What was he trying to prove? That he was living a good life? Just being here on this ferry, with the wind whipping against him, was proof enough that he was alive. He didn't need others to confirm this for him, but by posting the image he was inviting judgment, disappointment, failure. Why did *likes* matter? They didn't. He deleted the post.

Shortly after they'd passed Hjortø, Losman's cell pinged. He pulled the phone from his pocket and read the message.

hej losman. where are you? you ok?

He squinted at the screen, wondering who was texting him. He responded: *Who is this?*

it's me, caroline.

Losman's eyes widened. How did she get his phone number? He wrote back: *I'm on a ferry to Ærø. I stopped by your place, but you weren't there. I'm so sorry for yesterday!*

Her response was instantaneous: *how much do you remember?*

All of it! I was stuck in there the entire time.

where is *there*?

My head. I'm never going to do that again, Caroline!

that's good. but i want to hear everything! when are you back?

Thursday.

He expected her to respond right away. When she didn't, he created a new contact for her and slipped his phone back into his pocket. She must've gotten his number from Kat. She wasn't angry, she was curious, and she wanted to see him again. That she'd actively sought him out made him giddy.

In a fine mood, he jerked his head, cleared his throat, and stood at the railing to watch the ferry approach Ærøskøbing. With its dense cluster of traditional brick houses capped with orange terracotta roofs, the city resembled Svendborg or any Danish town he'd ever visited. As it docked, the big, grumbling engine churned the water into a foamy lather. Gulls swooped, screeching. When the ferry was at rest, Losman grabbed his stuff and disembarked. According to his phone, his Airbnb on Nørregade—listed on the website as a "cozy, charming house with a view of the sea"—was a 12-minute walk. To get there, he headed up Vestergade.

But first he stopped at Netto, the discount grocery store, and filled a bag with provisions that would get him through to Thursday.

Vestergade was like something out of a travel guide: a narrow cobblestone street bordered on either side by low, two-story brick rowhouses painted yellow or orange or ochre. The cobblestones were uneven, and as Losman hiked down the street an elderly woman wearing khaki shorts and a tank top—her tanned, leathery skin furrowed with wrinkles—bicycled slowly past him, bouncing over the ruts. She wore no helmet, and her hair was piled in an elegant chignon, making her look like the type of woman who enjoyed sailing with her husband while listening to classical music and drinking flutes of champagne.

The little yellow cottage Losman had rented was every bit as charming as the website had indicated. No false advertising here. After punching in the code to retrieve his key from the lockbox and letting himself in, he set his pack and Netto bag down in the entrance hall and toured the rooms. It was a cramped house with a galley kitchen and a kind of arthouse décor, with clay pots dangling from hooks over the sink and stove, landscape paintings depicting the same rolling hills he'd sped past on the train, and aromatic sprigs of flowers emerging from a ceramic vase on the thick oaken dining table. The bedrooms were refrigerator cool and smelled of mothballs, as if he were the first guest of the season and the cottage hadn't been properly aired out. There was a handwritten note next to the vase. "*Velkommen til Feriehuset!*" it read, followed by a printed list of instructions, dos and don'ts, and suggestions for places to visit while on the island.

Losman opened the French door and stepped onto the small patch of yard to gaze upon the bright, shiny blue water of the Little Belt. Less than seventy-five yards away, a group of shiny white sailboats with lowered sails lay tethered in the harbor, and a dozen or so squawking gulls took flight. The sun was a low, pinkening orb balanced on the edge of the horizon like a bobber; dusk was a glowing, fiery blend of reddish orange, making the harbor and the tiled roofs behind him sparkle. If only he could capture this light, take it home with him, he could relive this moment always. Maybe he could even give it to Caroline as a gift, something for her to paint. She would love it here, he thought.

The setting sun also reminded him of the time, and his hunger. All he'd eaten since breakfast was a *tebirkes* and a banana. As he was returning to the house, his cell phone pinged. It was Caroline again.

finally heard from Simon Jakobsen, she wrote. *he told me Kramer had a daughter named Anna in Aarhus.*

Who is Simon Jakobsen?

the carpenter's son. remember, in Kramer's apt?

Oh, right. How did he find out Kramer had a daughter in Aarhus?

i don't know, but I looked her up and called her. that's why I stopped at your place.

Losman smiled, delighted to have this new method of communication with Caroline. This flurry of text messages seemed to be elevating their friendship to another, uncharted level. He set his phone on the dining table to retrieve his groceries and carried the heavy Netto bag to the kitchen counter. He began putting the items in the fridge: a loaf of rye bread, a log of cheddar cheese, cherry tomatoes, coffee, smoked salmon, a can of mackerel in tomato sauce, OJ, a six pack of a local beer called Ærø Gylden, and Apollinaris water. He popped the can of mackerel and scooped the fish onto a slice of bread.

He sat down and took a cool swig of beer. *Is she as crazy as her father?* he wrote. Like a lovestruck dork, he stared at the screen until the three little dots appeared to indicate she was responding.

no, she's very nice. she told me Kramer was cremated. she invited the two of us to help scatter his ashes.

She did? Why?

I told her we were friends with him.

But we weren't.

we were as much as we could be. we tried.

You tried. When?

next saturday. it's his birthday.

Losman pictured an image of the calendar he'd tacked to the wall above his desk. Was he supposed to have Aksel next weekend? He typed his response,

In Aarhus?

no, Silkeborg. apparently, Kramer grew up there. do you want to come with me? Anna says we can spend the night at her house.

Losman typed madly, *Yes, I'd love to. I just need to check with Kat about Aksel.*

is it too much trouble?

No trouble at all! Count me in!

Losman hoped that he didn't sound too eager. He recalled what Kat said to him before the U2 show. *I'll owe you one.* Well, now she could pay up.

ok! i'll let her know we'll be there.

Great! he replied.

He stared at the screen, but this time she didn't respond. No matter. He shoved his cell into his pocket and went back inside, thrilled.

Silkeborg was a medium-sized city located in what was arguably one of the most beautiful regions in Denmark. It was surrounded by a clutch of lakes, and there was a vast tract of forest south of the city, the largest woodland area in the country. He recalled one hot summer, seven or eight years ago, when he and Kat had rented a cabin overlooking one of these lakes. For an entire week they'd hiked, rowed boats, and made love—once while skinny-dipping under a ghostly full moon; her body had shivered under his hands, and his had shivered under hers. That trip had solidified in Losman's memory as one of his fondest. Questions peppered him now: What would happen between him and Caroline in Silkeborg?

Could she be interested in him in spite of what he'd done?

Why not? Yes, why *not*? He would think positive thoughts for a change. She had seen him naked, had literally spoon-fed him like a baby, and yet she didn't hate him. He would have to be open about his Tourette, would now have to present himself to her *figuratively* naked. He couldn't—and wouldn't—hide that part of himself from her.

Losman devoured his dinner. He emptied his backpack on a bed, more like a cot, in one of the rooms and grabbed *Oryx & Crake* and his notebook. He got himself another beer and carried everything outside to breathe the salty sea air, to suck it deep into his lungs. Off in the distance came the otherworldly cackle of the gulls. He opened his book and began to read. The combination of cold beer, the still-warm rays of fading sunlight on his face, and his pleasant, post-texting-Caroline-mood made him positively euphoric, and he lost himself in the novel. He loved Atwood's sentences, the way they flowed inexorably onward, like a river to the sea. Translating *her* would be a delight. Her turns of phrase, her vivid characters, and her masterful ability to construct a perfectly plausible world out of disparate parts—all inspired Losman's imagination.

Aksel, Tourette Syndrome, BhMe4, Caroline, Pelin, Kat, his mother and father. Jens. Hell, even *Kramer*. This small constellation of satellites that orbited him, or maybe it was the other way around? He focused on them. Because if he could find the red thread that linked them all together, he was certain he had a story to tell. But was it a novel? Was it a memoir? And where would he begin?

He pulled his Moleskin notebook from his pocket and clicked his pen. His mind—aided by alcohol—raced with ideas, and he jotted them down before they slipped away, the tip of his pen scratching the surface of the paper. *Could* he write again? Did he have a story people would read?

Why did that even matter? Whether anyone read it or not, his story was his story.

After freewriting a few pages of notes—half-formed sketches, images, and sentences that ended abruptly, a trail to nowhere in particular but a trail nonetheless—Losman put his pen down and reread what he'd written. Even incomplete as it was, he knew that he'd captured the essence of *something*, though just what that something was lay beyond his grasp. A swooping gull screeched bloody murder, and he glanced up to find it tracing a low trajectory over the water, its white feathers ablaze in a shimmery halo of light. Losman felt a chill. The sun had vanished below the cottage behind him, and he was now seated in a broad stripe of cool shade.

He went back inside.

In his mind, Losman saw the arc of the story beginning with Caroline and the day she came to tell him about Kramer's fall. That was a good place to begin, with Kramer's demise. He didn't want to end with the scene in Silkeborg, because that would make it seem like a romantic comedy with a happy ending. Happy endings were great in real life, but they were terrible in books. Besides, he didn't know if there would be a happy ending.

No, it was best to end his story with ambiguity. That was always better. The truth of the matter was that he didn't know where his story would end any more than anyone knew how *any* story would end. On that score he was in the dark, like everyone else.

But it was time to begin. To prepare, he cleared his throat and shook his head repeatedly, until spittle flew from his mouth. He stripped off his pants and sat at the dining table in his briefs, pen in hand, notebook open. Finally, he was ready. He turned his head toward the front door of the cottage as if expecting Caroline to materialize there.

~~Losman was startled~~

He wrote this line but crossed it off immediately. He would have to change his name, he realized, to hide the bits of memoir from the fiction. And Caroline's. And Kat's. And Pelin's. Everyone would have to have new names, new faces.

He started over.

Author's Note

A few years ago—well into my adulthood—I was diagnosed with Tourette Syndrome. For as long as I can remember, I've dealt with the kinds of motor and vocal tics Losman manages in this novel, using the same sort of coping mechanisms that he employs. From the moment I wake up in the morning to the moment I fall asleep at night, my tics are *always* there, lurking, a constant, irritating companion. Like Losman, I've always tried to hide these tics from others because I was (and continue to be) embarrassed by them. Also like Losman, in elementary school I experienced a humiliating classroom scene with a teacher who should have known better than to single out a student for public shaming. Likely as a result of this episode, I believed something was deeply wrong with me—that *I* was the problem. As an adult, I've learned to accept that I am not the problem. I have Tourette, but Tourette doesn't have me.

At the time my teacher called me out for disturbing the class, in the mid-1980s, I was completely on my own with my self-abasing feelings. I had no one to turn to for help. No one ever discussed Tourette Syndrome, unless it was to satirize the poor people who express their Tourette by uttering obscene or inappropriate words in public. This is called coprolalia, and it's the version of Tourette that gets the most public attention. Because my vocal and motor tics were relatively tame by comparison—especially once I learned to hide them—I imagine this was the reason my parents never took me to see a specialist when I was young. I don't blame them for this; it was a different era. The Tourette Association of America was founded in 1972 with a mission of educating the public and providing support for families, but I didn't even know it existed until 2017, when the neurologist who diagnosed me suggested I reach out to find a support group. Things have certainly improved considerably for kids with Tourette since my childhood, thanks in large measure to the work of the Tourette Association of America.

Despite some deliberate similarities, *The Book of Losman* is decidedly a work of fiction, however. I am *not* Losman, and Losman is not me.

I started writing this book because I am fascinated by memory, and in particular with the idea that long-lost memories can be restored to you. Before I started writing *Losman*, I'd spent ten years researching and writing 17 drafts of a longer, darker novel that, in the end, my then agent, Mark Falkin, could not sell despite his best efforts. It's a tough business, publishing, and Mark did a great job getting my book in front of many of the best editors around. With *Losman*, I wanted to tell a lighter and funnier story where I could draw from my own experiences, with Denmark, with translation, with Tourette. I didn't want to spend ten years writing the novel either; in the end, it took only five. Mark provided good early feedback on *The Book of Losman*.

I'm not a neuroscientist, and you have to suspend your disbelief a wee bit with BhMe4 and the clinical trial in this novel. This is the beauty of fiction. You can package odd bits into a story so long as the world you create has a believable inner logic at its core. I hope you've found *The Book of Losman* believable enough to keep turning pages. Over the years it took to draft this novel, a number of wonderful people read the manuscript in its various stages, giving me and the story their time, energy, and keen eyes. It's a far better book now than it was after the first draft.

Let's start with Bill Hall, a professor of medicine at the University of Rochester School of Medicine. He gave me one solid piece of advice that, I confess, I decided not to heed. He suggested an alternative to how Losman comes to the clinical trial. After weighing my options and really considering *what* I was writing, a speculative fiction, I decided to keep my version of events. If there is any criticism to be leveled by neuroscientists at what I've done here, including factual errors, the criticism should be directed at me and me alone. I *did* tone down the number and duration of Losman's erections—another bit of advice from Bill—but I couldn't bring myself to get rid of them completely for reasons inherent in the narrative.

Dr. Peter Morrison of the University of Rochester Medical Center was the one who finally diagnosed me in 2017, and he gave me a good deal of insight into my Tourette along the way. He did not read this book, but I hope, if he ever does, he will appreciate my effort.

Thank you to my writing group, TBK, writers and readers of the highest order: Jess Fenn, Sejal Shah, and Stephen West. I've always struggled with expressing my most heartfelt emotions, and hugging people usually requires effort—I get anxious just thinking about it—but I'm truly grateful for the trust and friendship I've found in this group. Sharing your new writing with others is a vulnerable experience, much like being naked in public, I imagine, but this group makes it easy. I could hug you all.

Andrew Ervin, an extraordinary writer and friend, provided outstanding feedback and encouragement at a time when I was in dire need of both. He also enthusiastically offered to write the blurb you see here on this book. I can't begin to tell you what that means to me.

Stephen G. Eoannou, Owen King, Edan Lepucki, Ravi Mangla, Rion Amilcar Scott, and Daniel Torday also read the book and provided blurbs. I admire the hell out of their writing, and it's an honor to have their words appear on my novel. Thank you all.

An early version of chapter one appeared in the *Green Mountains Review* (volume 30 number 2). Thank you to fiction editor Jensen Beach, also a fantastic writer and translator of Swedish literature, for publishing the story.

My fellow Danish translators (and writers!) Mark Mussari and Misha Hoekstra provided an extra set of eyes on my American-in-Denmark view of Copenhagen. They too provided wonderful blurbs.

Stacey Freed, a fine journalist and writer, read an early version of the novel and provided me with solid feedback. Thank you, Stacey.

I want to be perfectly clear that I adore Denmark, my wife's native country and my second home, and no Danish writer was harmed in the making of this book. Niels H. Petersen is a complete fabrication, a bombast of the highest order, his novels deliberately outlandish in the way characters in American television sitcoms are deliberately outlandish. But I do want to acknowledge one Danish writer whose work has had an outsize and positive influence on me and *The Book of Losman*: Simon Fruelund. Simon was one of the first writers I translated, and our conversations on stories, language, word choice, and a host of other topics have all sharpened my vision. Not surprisingly, his feedback on this novel was spot on. With Simon's permission, chapter one is a retelling, a *reimagining*, of his story "Kramer" from his collection *Milk* (translated by me and also published by SFWP). I've also scattered little Easter eggs throughout this novel from each of his books I've translated, most notably from *Milk* and *The World and Varvara* (Spuyten Duyvil, 2023). Simon is a writer more Americans should read, so I encourage you to get ahold of his books ASAP.

Thank you to Andrew Gifford, SFWP's visionary founder and publisher. Andrew took a chance on *Milk*, a translated short story collection—one of the hardest kinds of books to sell—and I am truly grateful that he took the same chance on *The Book of Losman*. During the past two plus decades, SFWP has demonstrated time and again that it is an outstanding indie press, one of the best there is. Adam al-Sirgany, my editor at SFWP, is a fantastic close-reader who really poured himself into these pages. Thank you for seeing what needed to be done and improving this book, Adam. Gwen Grafft, SFWP's graphic designer, nailed the cover in only three takes; it's exactly what I'd hoped for, Gwen, so thank you.

A huge thank you to my wife, Pia Møller, and our son, Esben. Pia read an early draft of this novel and provided valuable nuggets of ideas (and encouragement) at every stage of its creation. It wouldn't be what it is today without her. Esben, meanwhile, helps me get out of my head and keeps me grounded in reality. That's kind of important—most of the time.

Finally, last but certainly not least, I want to thank you for reading this book. I'm truly humbled and grateful that you dedicated a few hours of your life to Losman's story. Since you've come this far, if it's not too much trouble, please consider leaving or posting a review on any of the platforms you use each day. Or tell your friends.

A little love goes a long way.

—August 24, 2023

About the Author

K.E. Semmel is a writer and translator. His fiction and nonfiction have appeared in *Ontario Review, Lithub, The Writer's Chronicle, The Southern Review, Washington Post,* and elsewhere. He has translated more than a dozen novels from Danish, and is a former Literary Translation Fellow from the National Endowment for the Arts. *The Book of Losman* is his first novel. Find him online at kesemmel.com and on Twitter/X at @kesemmel.

Translated by K.E. Semmel

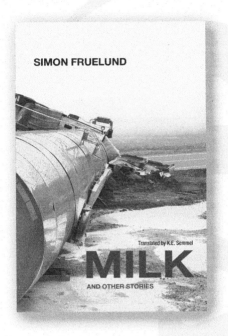

"This consistently beautiful book has a quietness that recalls the stark Danish countryside."
— *Publishers Weekly*

"Fruelund is a master of the short form, importing some designs from our own Raymond Carver, applying them to the interstices of the European everyday, and making them his own. The title story is a masterpiece in miniature."
— Alan Cheuse, *All Things Considered*

Find out more by scanning below:

About Santa Fe Writers Project

SFWP is an independent press founded in 1998 that embraces a mission of artistic preservation, recognizing exciting new authors, and bringing out of print work back to the shelves.

  @santafewritersproject | @SFWP | sfwp.com